Finding Solace

by

C.L. Scholey

Ancient Origins Book 2

Finding Solace

Contact Information: info@thewildrosepress.com

Cover Art by *Kristian Norris*

The Wild Rose Press, Inc.
PO Box 708
Adams Basin, NY 14410-0708

Visit us at www.thewilderroses.com

Publishing History
First Scarlet Rose Edition, 2017
Print ISBN 978-1-5092-1750-2
Digital ISBN 978-1-5092-1751-9

Published in the United States of America

**One man and woman will travel to the ends
of a handful of Earths for love…**

Menace released her and hovered over her. Solace knew better than to trace his many tattoos. The images were haunting. Not all were faces, some images were of a cherished item, something of significance left behind and etched onto skin. His tale was a sad one he had told her when they first met, wanting her to know everything about him. The sacrifices he and his people endured hurt his heart.

The drawings stopped many years ago when the last of Menace's tribe was hunted to death. He was certain his fate would be the same, and he developed a cavalier attitude toward death—whatever came would come. He continued to live, and soon his thoughts tormented him, building to a fury so intense he became the name he despised—Menace.

The last of his people, he roamed until finding Doom's village. He was welcomed. Solace knew he refused to sacrifice again. It didn't matter. The shame was Doom's to bear. It was his village. Menace turned his rage to hunting. Nothing was safe when he walked the jungle, and the dinosaurs learned to give him and his unpredictable rage a wide berth.

"How can you love a man like me?"

Too late, he'd seen where her gaze rested. "How can I not?"

Dedication

Special thanks to Janet S. for her knowledge on deerskin and her endless patience and friendship, greatly appreciated. As well as Mike for the knife tip and for answering my sometimes endless questions.

Chapter One

Trembling, Solace watched his approach. His sheer muscle mass rippled his naked thighs. He was bare-chested, and she longed to run her hands over his wide expanse of intricate bumps and trace his magnetic, complex tattoos. His perfect hands were balled to fists. Those hands could rip the ribcage of a velociraptor apart, she saw him do it, and they could bring the gift of pleasure to life over soft, eager skin. Closer, closer he stalked, while she lay pinned by his gaze alone. The fur on the large raised platform beneath her was warm and soft, his bed, now hers, too. The fibers tickled her bare backside. She curled her fingers into the warmth in anticipation.

The first time she laid eyes on this man was her undoing. Solace had never encountered a more perfect male. Only on this strange ancient planet was there ever the epitome of maleness, brute strength, and determination. Solace tingled knowing he was all hers, and she was his.

Menace was his name, and it suited him. A glare cast in any direction could send powerful men fleeing. His fists, sledgehammer-sized power behind a blow, could be wielded with meticulous accuracy. So fierce was his hunger for life it showed in everything he did. Menace moved with the grace of a huge cat, a saber tooth, on the prowl. Lithe, strongminded, passionate, his sleek skin already turned a tawny, almost golden color from the new spring sun. The pads of his feet on the strewn thick fur carpets covering a stunning amber floor continued forward. Solace remembered hearing something about a river of tea flowing into the oceans to create amber.

Solace wasn't afraid of his approach. The pounding of her erratic heartbeat thundered within her breast. Her legs ached to spread for him, but she remained immobile, her breath small pants, her gaze devouring his body. Menace settled beside her on the bed, his huge frame dwarfed hers but never to intimidate. His warmth was heavenly. He lifted a hand to run his fingers through her tresses. Her light-colored hair slipped over his knuckles, just starting to tan as the season changed to spring.

"What are you thinking?"

His voice was all sexy hunger, deep, throaty, rumbling like an anticipated thunderstorm, and filled with interest. Menace was fascinated with everything she did. Wherever she went, he was close—a good thing in the primitive ancient world where she now resided. Hybrid dinosaurs roamed the planet, the best of the best, the biggest, strongest predators, ever known; at least to her. Her planet Earth never encountered the likes of the many mutated creatures. Death was near every moment Solace wandered from the safety of the village. But not now, now she was in Menace's sights, and his gaze devoured her. Her thoughts for a moment turned to sorrow as she answered his question. Though she had been thinking about his perfect beauty, her mind was always a heartbeat away from a sad thought. Her musings never far from his magnificence, she played a fateful day over within her mind. The day she met him and the occurrence right before.

"I was wondering how the children are, where they went. The ones who went through the sinkhole with me at the daycare on my planet Earth. I think about them every day, wondering, worrying, and hoping they are safe. When the ceiling opened above us, it was surreal then horrifying. All of them three and under. Their poor parents. We all suddenly vanished without a trace. I'll never know. I'll never see them again."

Not a day went by she didn't wrack her brains searching to see if she failed them as one by one they were sucked upward into the dark inky sinkhole. Tiny faces, reaching hands, cries of surprise, helpless loss. As always her eyes filled with tears she was unwilling to shed, the wetness on her cheeks would make the loss that much more real while the hurt was indescribable. She thought the children were safe with her. The sinkholes seemed to be in different areas. All were caught unaware as the eerie phenomenon began growing worse but she was in a daycare. Nothing bad was ever thought to occur where tiny children laughed and played peek-a-boo. Toy play mats made a poor blanket of false security. Solace trembled.

"Please stop. It's been months, sweetness. No other village has heard about the little ones. I'm certain they're safe somewhere else. We must try to think positive. We go into battle tomorrow. You need to be thinking straight."

He was right. She needed her mind to be in the here and now. It had been months since the devastating sinkhole sent her to this planet, this alternate Earth where dinosaurs walked the surface. Upright hybrid dinosaurs that could think and kill, the Neandersauri wanted humans from Solace's Earth. Her friend Clarity claimed they wanted the intelligence to create space flight. They had to be destroyed before the villagers were killed. It was only a matter of time before the hybrids would be the only thinking species on the planet if war wasn't waged. Over the long winter months, Solace and the others made weapons and learned how to use them.

Clarity and Solace killed many hybrids during the village winter hibernation when Menace and the other villagers slept, but more were coming. Death lurked everywhere on the planet. No meteor destroyed the dinosaurs here as they had on Solace's Earth. There were no volcanos or ice age melt to separate continents. There was no place to escape to, there was no flight—only fight. The once-dying villagers found hope with Clarity and now Solace. Her father was military, and Solace would do him proud by bringing her game tomorrow.

"Come back to me," Menace said as he traced her cheek with a strong finger.

Solace slipped from her reverie. "We used all the condoms for our bomb balloons."

"Then let's make a baby."

"Before war?"

"My entire life I've been at war with my thoughts. What we do tomorrow will be a relief."

What he said was true. If she were to die tomorrow, taking a piece of him to have with her always would be a comfort. If there might be the slightest chance of conception there was that little bit more to strive harder for victory.

"I love you, Menace." Solace took his finger from her face to kiss the tip. "The first time I saw you, I knew you would be the man to love. Your eyes say so much about you. Your soul is on display, and I am honored to be with such a man."

Menace found her in the forest appearing unconscious after her fall through the sinkhole. The ride through inky darkness was a hell like no other. Her body had bounced on impact when she hit the ground then settled. At first, she lay stunned watching one of the biggest men she had ever seen fight a raptor. A dinosaur. An unthinkable idea, to battle something that should be extinct. She lay crumpled on her side, her cheek pressed against an earth floor, the scent raw, ancient, and unfamiliar. She wasn't certain she was dreaming. The clash was intense. Man against beast. Menace fought with passion, he was very much the warrior she thought him to be, that he looked to be. A final blow with a huge sword sank into the beast's chest and down it went. Menace yanked the weapon free, and as Solace went under, succumbing to the darkness after her ride from hell, she watched his leather moccasins approach. Eyelids fluttering. Not a day passed when she cast her grateful gaze onto him. He taught her how to survive in his world. More importantly he gave her a reason to live. Menace wouldn't allow her to sink into despair.

When Solace woke the first time in Menace's home she was naked on a platform, his bed. A thick fur beneath her and a slight fur was settled to her hips and Menace sat beside her. His tone, so sweet and endearing, he told her about his world, about him. At first, pinned by his size, but not weight, she was unmoving. The entire time he didn't sit ogling her, his gaze was earnest. He spoke until he seemed as naked as she was. He bared everything, including his heart. The same sincere expression gripped her this moment.

"There is so much more to love than emotions. There is taste." He leaned over to press his lips to hers for a moment. "I can taste love on your lips. I can feel love with my fingers." The pads of his digits traced a line from her shoulder to her hip. "I can tell you I love you because I do. I can see the words float across your beautiful face, the dazzle of light in your eyes. You are dipped in sunshine. I will always have light if I have you. You are the dawn of each day, sweetness. There is no cold when your sight warms my heart."

Solace melted with each word. "You make love with your mouth in so many ways."

Menace nestled his face against her throat. His breath washed over her. A hand gripped her hair to tilt her neck back. He suckled her flesh making her heart leap. The pressure of his hand cupped her ass pulling her closer. For a moment his grip intensified, her breasts were squished to his chest. She gasped.

"Can you feel me?" he whispered.

"Yes."

The heat from his arousal seared her to her bones. Every inch of him was hard and hot, alive with desire for her. Menace pressed her back against the furs, sinking her into softness. He sat up to straddle her. Both hands found her breasts and kneading them, his thumb pads roamed her nipples. Small hard buds formed. With deliberate determination, he leaned over her. His mouth captured a bud and suckled until she wanted to scream. Warm wetness built between her thighs as he continued his exquisite torture. Solace cried out when his finger found her bud as she spread her legs.

"Can you feel my love for you? Can you hear my heart beating for yours?" he whispered.

"Yes." She was breathless.

Her eyes wide, she glanced up. Solace was safe from the incredible monstrosities of the planet while nestled in this home. His home was buried beneath mammoth and mastodon bones and strange meteor rocks that landed harmlessly and were harvested for their powerful glowing rays. It didn't matter what noise they made as they loved one another, she was in a soundproof fortress deep within the ground. The ceiling above was domed and twenty feet high while they remained secure. The walls were rock interwoven with a dark substance. An intricate pattern waist height was amber. A simple touch from warm flesh made the rock glow.

Solace grew warmer. Menace's fingers danced across her belly. Not far from the bed of piled furs was a round rock shelter with glowing fire. A breeze blew for ventilation. Solace didn't know from where, she didn't care. At the moment, she was safely losing her sanity to a man whose mouth could make love in fascinating ways.

Her breast disappeared past his lips, and she smiled as she wondered if her nipple tickled his throat. He stretched his body over hers, lower to continue to suckle. The finger he delved into her heat surprised her for a mere second. His hands were large. A pumping finger was prelude to something larger yet to come. Another finger was added and she squirmed. She cupped his bald head with a hand and moved against his now slippery fingers.

Menace released her and hovered over her. Solace knew better than to trace his many tattoos. The images were haunting. Not all were faces, some images were of a cherished item, something of significance left behind and etched onto skin. His tale was a sad one he had told her when they first met, wanting her to know everything about him. The sacrifices he and his people endured hurt his heart.

The drawings stopped many years ago when the last of Menace's tribe was hunted to death. He was certain his fate would be the same, and he developed a cavalier attitude toward death—whatever came would come. He continued to live, and soon his thoughts tormented him, building to a fury so intense he became the name he despised—Menace.

The last of his people, he roamed until finding Doom's village. He was welcomed. Solace knew he refused to sacrifice again. It didn't matter. The shame was Doom's to bear. It was his village. Menace turned his rage to hunting. Nothing was safe when he walked the jungle, and the dinosaurs learned to give him and his unpredictable rage a wide berth.

"How can you love a man like me?"

Too late, he'd seen where her gaze rested. "How can I not?"

Menace ran a hand across his chest. "Never again. Never again will I mourn the loss of people who should have been better protected. My villagers fell while leaving me to roam alone. My heart aches for the destruction of so many."

Solace took his wrist and placed his hand over her heart. "Live in here until you can bear to live inside of you."

A small smile twitched his lips. They were rare gifts. "If I move in, you'll need a kick-ass dinosaur to evict me. I am told I'm strong."

Strong? There was no one more powerful.

"I'll take my chances handsome."

The nudge of a knee spread her thighs further. The tip of his cock slid ever so gently into her heat making certain she was ready.

"All of me is wet," she whispered. She wiggled her hips and winked at him.

"Then I best not keep you waiting."

His plunge was sharp, hard and he was thicker than ever. He was as much a thing of beauty as he was a beast. Menace was the perfect male. Ancient and vulnerable, powerful, gentle, he loved her like no man ever had or would again. Solace clung to him. Her arms weren't long enough to wrap around his astoundingly broad back.

Sharp claps of thunder reached her ears as he connected against her. His love-making embarked her into thought likening him to the elements. He moved fast and furiously. When the storms came to the planet, she watched him race with the ground lightning, his devil-may-care attitude. Nothing was faster than Menace, not even the Mother Nature who ruled here. Passion was how he survived, he was a man filled with purpose. She was at this moment his survival. She lifted her legs to wrap around his waist and hung tight. Menace was the rumble in the skies, the thunder between her thighs.

Gasping, her breath caught. He slipped a hand under her ass to make her move faster. A quick flip and she was in his arms, off the bed, both hands on her ass he pressed her to the hard rock of the wall, connecting them with a thump. She was pinned and immobile, his hands now free became a life of their own. He showed no mercy, and Solace was grateful. He gathered her wrists in one hand and pinned them high over her head jutting her breasts forward. His lips sucked hers, her throat, her cheeks.

The warmth of the surface behind her heated her ass and back. She was held easily. The passion in his gaze burned her face with want and need. She could feel the pounding of his heart, see the pulsing at his throat. Wild, untamed, raw desire commanded every inch of her to become one with him.

She felt the fast wave sweep over her when she came. Shivering to her toes, Solace cried out his name as he bucked harder, then harder still until she thought her bones would crack. His cock was hard and slick, his ass cheeks contracted with each motion showing defining muscle as her head slipped to his shoulder with exhaustion. She was building again, and the fear of an unknown tomorrow made her warrior reckless with want. Her quivering legs began to slip. There was no escape. His now intense expression pinned her to the wall when she leaned back to gather air into lungs desperate to fill. His growling pants for breath bathed her face as his teeth clenched.

"I will live in you forever," he ground out.

She wondered if he really did seek entry into her flesh through his maleness, his cock a battering ram to knock down her walls and allow the proverbial Trojan horse inside. She was sinking, her breath cut short. The power of her surrendering to Menace tightened her insides wanting to capture him within her forever. Menace roared his release, pulled her from the wall, and flopped them back onto the bed. She gasped in huge amounts of air, her fingers curled into the fur of the bed. Menace lay half over her with his head resting on her belly. When he chuckled, she was startled. The sound another rare gift and she wondered what brought it on. She cast a glance to where his gaze was settled. The rock wall glowed with her imprint.

"Well shit, how long will that last? My ass as big as day all lit up like a moon. *Oh my God.* I'm mooning us."

"I kinda like it. An in-your-face-take-that, bitches."

Solace groaned. "Do not open any doors until that butt imprint is gone. It's huge, a flying saucer that's been stung by a bee and not an EpiPen in sight."

"Your ass is perfect."

Menace pulled her against his chest. She wiggled her bottom against him. He chuckled again, and she could feel the rumbling sensation.

"Stop checking out my ass."

"All right, but that's not what you said a while ago. Sleep sweetness. We have a busy day ahead of us."

At this moment she was safe. Menace was right. Who knew what tomorrow would bring, but failure wasn't an option. She hoped the fates were on board with that.

Chapter Two

The villagers converged in the meeting hall underground. Doom, their leader, stood on a sturdy wooden table that ran almost the length of the hall to accommodate all when they gathered for a meal. The high domed ceiling was a few feet above his formidable six foot six height, two hundred eighty pounds. Menace wasn't as large but a close second. Doom favored knee-length deerskin pants, his weapons attached to his belt. Most of the men were dressed in a similar fashion.

Solace and the other women wore soft deerskins. The hides were warm and water resistant, not altogether waterproof. The soft leather was breathable and stretched to form fit the body. The fine, thin looking articles were deceptive at first glance. The material was strong and the deer was a favorite to hunt. Solace was surprised in this ancient world of dinosaurs the animals did well in herds. Despite Solace and Clarity's attempts at an upgrade, everyone wore leather booties that formed to the feet after time. The material was from a thicker hide of a mammoth mastodon mix, fur side turned in for warmth, water-resistant, sharp stick and rock proof, all in all sturdy if not stylish. During the winter months, the booty was made higher and stuffed with added fur fibers or grass.

Inside, the hall quieted immediately and Doom took a deep breath before beginning. The speech was one Solace was used to, a pep talk to soldiers before battle she'd heard her father practice enough, but she could tell others were moved by Doom's passion. Doom's chest, built a bit bigger than Menace, was intricately tattooed, more so than Menace. Each mark was a sacrifice, an offering of a human life the hybrids demanded for the safety of Doom's people in return. Today that would end. There would be no more sacrifices, no more tattoos would magically appear to identify the fallen. It was time to fight for all life. No more would Doom walk unsuspecting humans into the forest jungle and allow the Neandersauri easy pickings.

"You all know what to do. You all know why we must not fail and we will not fall." The people cheered. "Remember there is more danger out there than the hybrids. When blood is drawn the meat eaters will come. Strike hard, strike fast, and move on. I have faith in you. We will be victorious. Watch out for the raptors, we all know this time of year is volatile when the hybrids hunt. Their deep sleep makes them ravenous and unpredictable. Normally, they would expect all villagers to remain inside their dwellings. They are in for a surprise. Is everyone armed?" Doom shouted.

With a roar, swords lifted in affirmation. Solace was positive she could see the pulses throbbing at every neck near her in fear and anticipation. What they were about to do was unprecedented. The hybrids were used to being dominant. Today *they* would be the ones to die, not the villagers or the humans they'd found. The only ones not fighting were the youngest children except Luke, an eight-year-old boy. Kiki, his fifteen-year-old sister wanted him where she could see him. She knew if he was left alone, he would follow. The boy was prone to mischievous behavior. Nina, thirteen and Em, eight, and four-year-old twins, were hidden in the hibernating room with the others, and a very protesting Flight, a five-year of Solace's Earth planet, where the room was locked from the inside. There were few other children who were meek and not of Solace's world. Solace knew those little ones would stay put, theirs was not an arguing nature.

"Don't go," Blue, one of the twins protested. He wrapped little arms around Solace's neck clinging tight.

"We will be back soon. I promise you," she whispered into his ear and she squeezed him to her before letting go. She gazed at Cole, Blue's twin. His solemn round eyes gazed back woefully. Solace ruffled his hair and cupped his chin. "Keep your brother out of trouble." Blue was the alpha of the two. Cole nodded.

"Hurry home," Nina said, she took a hand of each twin and Solace watched the door close. In the last few months Solace had come to love these children. She vowed not to fail them, she settled open hands onto the door for a brief moment wanting to stay and protect them, and yet knowing every available sword was needed.

"They'll be fine." Menace placed a hand onto her shoulder and guided her away.

The bulwarks, massive dire wolf and cave bear mixes, were used to watching the village but Muffin, a female bulwark, was locked in the room with the children and Bubble-gum, who was a Rottweiler, Saint Bernard, standard poodle mix and the children. One troublesome and impish pint sized T-rex, belonging to Luke, nipped tails of the other bulwarks until he was chased off on a squeal of mock terror.

"Move out," Doom yelled.

A sense of peaceful, yet fiery resolve was in the air. Every available man, woman and a few children held swords, knives, and had access to crude homemade bombs. The explosives were hidden in strategic areas highly accessible if you knew where to look. The hybrids would have no clue what they were if they stumbled onto them or how they worked. The Neandersauri would be expecting the human sacrifices to be set free in the wooded jungle where they could be rounded up for slaughter. The beasts had no idea the villagers were armed and deadly, they trained well over the long winter before the long sleep and after. The villagers planned ahead, they were ready. Everyone filed out of different exits from their homes to begin the initial attack. Each site of engagement was littered with alternate escape routes.

"Stay on my six," Solace said to Menace.

"Your six what?"

"Stay on my ass."

"So now it's okay to keep your ass in sight?"

"At all times."

"Best war ever."

The villagers slipped through the trees in no less than pairs. Once the hybrids realized there was no sacrifice, they were the intended victims, the fighting began quickly. To Solace's left, a bomb blew, and she heard a sharp scream of pain and surprise. The normally cocky hybrids were used to being the dominants, used to being in charge. For many of their hybrid young, this was their first hunt for sacrifices. Instead, the youngsters fled in terror when they had never known fear in their lives. The balloons, condom and paper, carried bombs and a blinding substance. These were struck from their stationary elevated height tied to trees at intervals. They also contained a blue rock, glass-like, that could immobilize a victim with contact to the flesh. The substance was found on the beaches and collected with care. The glass could be shattered to allow small amounts to drop onto a victim. If the victim tried to brush the substance off, his or her hands would be paralyzed.

Menace was engaged in battle with two hybrids. The sword he held sliced back and forth sending the hybrids to their knees where he dispatched them immediately. Solace lost sight of Clarity, Doom's female. She caught a glimpse of a raptor pack dragging away the body of a hybrid. The hybrid was a special delicacy for the dinosaur. Normally, the creatures would be eating human remains.

More screaming followed as man and hybrid, and other animals got caught in the attacks. Solace watched a paper balloon explode carrying a liquid substance created by Clarity, her friend and fellow Earth comrade. Clarity was from Solace's Earth. Her scientific background was what convinced Doom and his villagers to fight, not only for their lives but for the lives of other humans. They had created swords with substances known to Clarity. As well as other knives and arrow tips able to penetrate the Neandersauri thick hides.

The hybrid hit by the liquid matter howled as his eyes burned from their sockets. Hybrid upright dinosaurs stood at least eight feet in height. Rainbow eyes and a triceratops frill ear to ear. Their bodies were bare in areas as well as colorfully feathered and furred in others. The creatures wore a simple wrap around their hips. All the fighting Neandersauri were males. Their broad chests were exaggerated muscles. Solace was aware of them, yet they managed to take her breath away each time she came into contact with one. The grayish frill lit with lively red colors, the patterns snake-like as they pulsed. Their solid bone mass was covered in heavily muscled hard flesh impenetrable with mere spears of stick or wood.

The hybrid, unable to see having been burned, faltered in agony not knowing where to turn, tripping then stumbling into a tree. Throwing his head back the beast took two long claws and sliced high on his chest. Solace almost vomited when the slits parted to reveal two dark eyes that blinked until growing accustom to the light. The hybrid could see again using the Neanderthal body within the hybrid body.

Solace knew about the double skeletal structure. She and Clarity had ripped open the chest of a dead hybrid. She never imagined she would find a full-fleshed creature within, smaller, dense, and humanoid. Heavy bones accommodated the outer structure of the heavy beasts. The inner humanoid creature was hairy, fully formed, a built-in furnace for the Neandersauri to survive in colder temperatures. They were scary as shit. To see the inner beast alive and blinking was mind-numbing. Were they two different entities working as one or was the entire body of the same soul, mind and thoughts?

Tremors gripped Solace. For a second all action ceased. The villagers had also come to know about the double structure of bones inside the hybrid, and now they knew there was also flesh, at least eyes to see with.

Edge, a huge villager, muscular, bald, ran forward and stabbed the beast in a new eye. The strangled scream proved the inner beast was vulnerable. As Edge withdrew his sword the hybrid fell. When another hybrid was burned at the ears, slits along the sides of its body under the arms were made. Solace couldn't see ears but she knew the hybrid was using the ones from within its body to hear.

The blast of a balloon hit with Kiki's arrow into the tall trees and the blue glass substance spattered over a hybrid who flopped to the ground and remained immobile. Solace knew the creature could see, hear and feel everything though its body couldn't move. Solace gagged when a raptor dragged it away to feast on its body while the hybrid still breathed. The gruesome sight of its entrails being exposed while it lived was horrifying and hard to look away from.

From behind her, Solace heard a strangled scream and spun to see Menace pull a sword from a hybrid, claws inches from her back. As Solace watched with wide eyes, Menace sliced a clawed hand from the beast. The inside limb, still intact and not severed at the wrist was exposed. Another slice at the elbow and the hand fell; it pulled itself along the earth floor until it settled.

For years Solace had heard of war; her father was a storyteller. They watched old wars fought in black and white, and her father would make funny noises as if to say 'nope, not how it happens'. She knew there would be gore but her father neglected to mention how much, the sight, the smell, the taste of fleshy sewage on the tip of her tongue. She was inhaling assault. Solace knew the scent of death, she had sliced into dead poisoned hybrids to make certain they stayed dead, but this was different. Fresh death. The rivers of blood flowed, undammed. There was twice as much coming from two body sources. Fury-filled anger raged, the likes she'd never seen or ever wanted to again. Her breath was torn from her throat then caught to settle like a stone in her chest.

Chaos gripped Solace's world. Solace could see Menace battling another hybrid demon. The Neandersauri stood eight feet high on its tall muscular legs. The older mature beast was swinging his huge claws trying to split Menace open. To her left Doom battled another. The villagers had learned well how to wield the swords Clarity made for them. Little Luke, only eight years old was back to back with his older sister Kiki. The smallest ninja of their troop swung his sword slicing the claws off a hybrid. At Luke's side was his pintsized T-rex friend, Rex. The small dinosaur, not much taller than Luke, lunged at the hybrid's throat with a large mutt of a dog from Earth dubbed Bubble-gum.

Solace reeled. Why was she seeing the dog? He should be locked in with the children. *Oh my God, the children.*

In the distance, she could make out Kiki's hyena friend, Bongo, and not far was Muffin, the villager's malevolent bulwark, the sweetest of the four hybrid bulwark creatures. Men and women from surrounding villages stood—and fell, with Doom's people. Other different dinosaurs besides raptors snuck in to take advantage of the fallen, hybrid and human. Some of the dinosaurs added their own roars and screams to the anarchy. The beasts came in all shapes and sizes, their DNA meshed with those of other deadlier dinosaurs to create creatures that never roamed Solace's Earth. War meshed with a gruesome fighting feeding frenzy.

Solace's heart skipped a beat while her gaze searched and when some of the younger children from Doom's village came into view. Earth children, from Solace's Earth. They were supposed to be staying in the safety of the domed homes with other children not of Solace's planet. The children were too small to wield real swords. The twins were running holding hands amidst the fight. She spotted Nina with little Em on her heels. She spied Clarity and Menace going after the children, their expressions full of horror. Her heart screamed in terror. Solace knew she needed to get to them. These were more children she couldn't bear to fail. Children she had grown to love.

I will not mourn another child.

The ground shook sending Solace to her knees as well as many other humans and hybrids. The raptors scattered with other dinosaurs. An earthquake to add terror to panic. The earth split with the glimpse of a black void, giving birth to a plane, and Solace sat on her ass mouth agape at the scene. In the ancient jungle of a planet similar to Earth the sight was breathtaking, terrifying. No meteor had ever crashed into this Earth. Hybrid dinosaurs and humans battled for dominance. It was imperative the hybrids didn't come near the plane, the creatures must never know of space voyage. Solace leapt to her feet, her fists balled as she pumped her legs for all she was worth. The battle raged harder as the hybrids gazed with awe, wanting this flying beast, salivating for the chance to study it. Solace saw the gazes of a few Neandersauri and knew a human stem cell memory they harvested into their systems with the sacrifices was flipped on. The boy, Flight, was screaming and running. It was his father's plane.

How can that be?

The child was adamant, and Solace raced to gather him up with the four-year-old fraternal twins. Cole had a death grip on his brother's hand. The plane touched down and the door flung wide. Solace's mind was racing. If this plane came through, it could go back to her Earth. The children were loaded with the injured and fallen teen, sixteen-year-old Nick. Nick the wild feral boy who saved children and loathed Doom with a passion after watching Doom lead his brother to the slaughter when Nick was only six. The boy survived on his own for years. The teen came to help keep his friends stay safe but it was obvious his arms, both long since broken and healed wrong, couldn't hold a sword.

Em, the eight year old was next into the plane though she glanced from Nick to Kiki who was fighting alongside her brother.

"Solace what about the others?" the girl cried out.

"Nick needs a hospital," Solace yelled over the plane's engine.

Solace's Earth children knew what a plane was. Em was followed by thirteen-year-old Nina who raced to Nick's side and glanced worriedly at Solace.

"You'll be fine," Solace shouted. "You can go home."

Nina yelled back something, but there was too much confusion and the girl was back too far in the plane. The plane, long and sleek, was a beacon of safety, Solace hoped. Flight was pulled onto his father's knee. The ground began to shake as the sinkhole started to close. The plane revved. Solace turned away. The children needed to be returned home; she'd done all she could for them. She hated to see them leave but they would be far safer on her Earth. Nick would finally be able to see a doctor, maybe he would get answers about his parents and if they were alive.

Anarchy raged. More hybrids were downed as they battled to reach the incredible sight. An object of tremendous value, the hybrids longed for flight and there it was, feet away. Clarity stood not far and held her hand out, she was disheveled, her face a mask of shock. Something had happened to her, Solace could tell. Something terrifying. Solace could see Menace as he raced toward her. In a few short months, he had become everything to her. Lover, friend, protector. Here was home with the man she loved beyond belief. She started to move toward him and smiled. Even with a battle raging everything would be fine as long as they were together.

Solace screamed when a man grabbed her from behind. He pulled her kicking and screaming into the plane. He looked past her to Clarity's shocked expression before shaking his head and slamming the door.

"We've no more room." Solace heard yelled. "We can't save them all and the sinkhole is closing."

"We got what we came for," was a shouted reply from the pilot.

Solace screamed for them to stop, she wanted out. They wouldn't let her near the door. She could see Menace through a window, his face a mask of horror, arm stretched reaching for her, racing for her. He was bellowing he loved her. The plane was only meant to save the children, Solace didn't need saving. She couldn't bear to see the little ones swallowed by a hole, but this was a *plane*. She had to get off.

"*Menace*," Solace screamed.

"I will find you." She saw him mouth the words as he dropped to his knees and the plane was airborne. His absolute look of agonized despair crumpled her.

Solace was tossed into a seat, a belt settled across her hips in haste. She shoved at the large man. He took her fear as shock and pushed her back none too gently.

"You'll be fine," he yelled. "This is a plane, not a human-eating demon."

"Let me off," she screamed. Her words fell on deaf ears as the man buckled in beside her and the pilot battled to keep the plane on track. The crying and yelling of the children was too loud. Solace couldn't make herself be heard, then it was too late.

The craft rose high before nose diving toward the earth and the rapidly closing sinkhole. Solace's guts fell as she watched the ground race closer. They descended into hell and all went dark. Silence ensued. Down they went into the bowls of an abyss. A sick scraping sounded as the sides of the plane hit walls, sparks flew lighting the interior in glimpses. Terrified faces gazed back at Solace and she knew they mirrored hers. The plane shot from the hole as it screeched to a close behind them. The engines sputtered and died. The plane leveled off as the wheels hit the bumpy ground. Rock formations and dingy colored shrubs flew by, it was daylight.

The man beside her stuck out his arm as she was bumped forward. He gripped the other side of her seat pressing her back. Solace closed her eyes and concentrated on breathing while she clung to her seat.

Teeth rattled, hers and others. The pounding of her heart ricocheted inside her ears. Clamping her teeth together helped her to think.

The plane swerved to the side, forming a circle. The move was the pilot's effort to slow it down. It came to a halt and everyone took a collective breath. Solace took note of the people on board. A tall man with a broad build stared back at her. He had short darkish hair, rugged good looks and wore tanned pants and a tan vest. He wasn't from Doom's village, but there was something primitive to his attire. He sprung forward and peered over the captain's head.

"Where the hell do you think we are now, Joe?"

"Your guess is as good as mine, Lochlan."

"Damn. I hope we finally landed somewhere we can understand." He gazed at Solace. "I'm Lochlan. What you're on is called a plane, so don't be scared."

"I know what a plane is." Though Solace tried, she couldn't keep the dry sarcasm from her tone. "My name is Solace, the children are Cole, his brother Blue, that's Em and Nina and the one unconscious is Nick. I'm guessing you all know Flight, by the name of Joey Jr." The boy grinned at her from his father's arms.

"Are you okay, buddy?" Joe asked his son.

"I knew you'd come, Daddy. I told them but they never had their listening ears on," Joey said.

"I'm Joe," the one holding his son began. "That's Lochlan, Bastian, and Tain." Solace wasn't certain who was who with the other two men from the flippant introduction.

"Besides the boy over there are any of you hurt?" Joe asked.

I'm dying, Solace was thinking and was about to

rage at Lochlan who'd basically kidnapped her. She was stopped by movement.

A huge black man went to open the door but was detained by Lochlan raising a hand. "Wait, Bastian. We better sit tight for a bit and check everyone over."

Solace unbuckled the belt at her hips and went to Nick. The sixteen year old was still unconscious, slumped in a corner with Em pressed to his side. His wounds weren't as bad as Solace first thought, it was the bump on his head that concerned her. She lifted his eyelids noticing they were responsive to light.

"Are any of you doctors?" she asked.

All gave a negative shake of their heads. Everyone turned when Nina screamed and raced into the arms of Lochlan. The surprised man had his arms to his sides until the girl screamed again. He pulled her tight. A massive snout was in the window and Solace shuddered when it snorted hot breath to fog the window inches from her face. Her heart began to pound at the ramifications gazing back at her. *This isn't my earth. Why isn't this my earth?*

"What is that?" Nina said, still howling. "That's not on Doom's planet."

"Look." Blue pointed.

Solace gazed at where the four year old was pointing. A herd of scutosaurus were curiously gazing at the plane. Massive turtle-like creatures munched bushes. The earth beneath their feet was a light color of brown. Balls of dust from the ground flew then settled when they moved.

"Crap," Bastian said. "Where there's a vegetarian there's bound to be a synapsid. Yep, shit, over there. A gorgonopsid."

"What's a gonogos?" Blue asked.

"Trouble," the last man, Tain, spoke.

The herd scattered when a beast crept into vision. Solace stared at it. Ten feet in length, long saber fangs and covered in patches of tawny colored hair matching the sandy dirt beneath its four feet.

"All righty boys, it's time to lock and load. I'm starving," Lochlan said. He disengaged Nina from his arms and sat her down in a nearby seat with a quick easy smile.

Solace grabbed his arm. "You can't go out there."

"Not yet. We'll let the dino do the dirty, then kill it when its victim is down. That way we don't waste as many bullets."

To each window they crept as the meat-eater charged its victim. Small faces in silent awe, eyes wide and round. Adults in anticipation of a meal. Plowing face first into the herbivore's side, the gorgonopsid took a bite causing a gaping hole, intestines swung to drag across the bloodied ground.

"Gross," Nina whispered.

"Cool," was Blue's reply.

"Nasty," Em said, while Cole nodded.

The reptile stumbled, tried to flee, then fell. A massive shake of the gorgonopsid head with its huge jaws clamped around the throat and the scutosaurus was dead. The rest of the herd remained a safe distance from the plane and meat eater. The dinosaur dove face first into the belly. When it came up for a breath, its muzzle was covered in dripping blood. It chewed, then tossed back its head to swallow.

"Well, that beast can consider itself field dressed. Time to go hunting," Lochlan said.

The pilot and three other men held their semi's tight, leaving the plane and, with caution, approached the pair of dinosaurs. The great beast dwarfed them and paid them no attention. Solace watched as the gorgonopsid ripped off another mouthful. Shots were fired. The gorgonopsid staggered, the food in its mouth plopped to the ground. The creature centered its gaze onto the four miniscule beings as though to take a better look and Solace swallowed hard. Another round of bullets exploded. The staggering beast's front legs buckled, ass in the air for only moments, it crashed to its side. Solace could feel the earth tremble and all four men seemed to jump then settle. Both dinosaurs were dead.

Joe took out a large knife and while the others watched for intruders both inside the plane and out, he sliced huge chunks. Tain shook out a plastic silver blanket and they piled the meat onto it dragging it back. Soon a fire was built and meat was roasting. Solace made a broth for Nick who woke from the noise of the guns. The teen glared at her but accepted the food. Outside, Joey, who refused to answer to the name Flight, sat next to his father. Em, Nina, and the twins opted to take their food after it was cooked into the plane to sit with Nick.

The day had been grueling for all of them. Joey fell asleep at his father's hip. Joe carried him into the plane. The children were tucked into seats for the night with thin blankets as the adults sat talking by the fire. Solace was passed a cup of steaming hot coffee. She knew the men meant well, thinking they saved her. All were pleasant and polite. Good with the other children. She needed to get home. This planet wasn't as safe as the last one if she could calculate the time period. Her emotions were torn in two. She desperately missed Menace, but the children needed her. Her emotions were a swirl of questions.

"Did you get to the last planet you picked us up on via earth?" Solace asked.

"If you mean the earth we began in with my plane the answer is no," Joe said. "And how do you know it's planets and not a vortex or different planes of existence we end up in?"

"I don't know. It's a guess, you might be right. How many places have you been to?" Solace asked.

"Five, well six counting here," Lochlan said.

"Joe here wanted his boy," Bastian said and clapped the man on the shoulder.

"We can't stay here," Lochlan said.

"No kidding, we need a place to fuel up soon. Next place we land better have something to juice up the plane." Joe sighed.

"What I wouldn't give for some sense of normalcy. By the way, I'm Tain." He was the last to introduce himself to Solace, though she'd guessed his name. Tall, blond, built and dangerous looking, his slight smile softened his rugged features. His eyes were as blue as the sky.

"I need to go back," Solace said.

"*What?*" From all four men.

"Menace is on the planet you took me from. You should have left me there with him." She settled her accusing gaze on Lochlan. Dark brown eyes widened in surprise.

"From what I saw you were battling for your lives. I felt like shit leaving the other woman there. Grabbing you was pushing it. If I could have gotten my hands on those two other kids instead I would have."

"I know what it must have looked like, but we were winning the battle and those two kids, Kiki and Luke, would never have left willingly either. You might have had a hand severed or been bitten, and not just by the children. The boy Luke and his older sister Kiki have lived on that planet for three years with the boy Nick, who by the way hates everyone. Clarity and Doom have made the children part of their lives, and they would die to protect them. So would I and Menace. I know Menace is alive and he will be worried for all of us. I was hoping you were taking us back to our Earth. I could have found the sinkhole that brought me to the other planet and returned. I could have gotten these kids to family. It's obvious you have no control over where you're going. Menace will be worried sick when I don't return."

"Why would you think we have control over sinkholes? Do I look like a magician? Menace? Who the hell names their kid Menace?" Bastian asked, his dark eyes wide.

"The same type of people who would name their son Doom. The world they live on is wild. Dinosaur hybrids, the Neandersauri, with a flesh and bone covered skeleton inside a flesh and bone covered skeleton. Hybrids, dinosaur slash Neanderthal slash crazy weird-as-shit things. A meteor never hit that Earth or plane of existence or whatever." Solace tossed the last of her meat in the fire. "It's imperative I get back after we get these kids to a safe place. If you don't know where we're going next we could end up anywhere. We need to get away from here, which I do

29

know."

"Even if we wanted to take you back, there's no guarantee we'll hit the right sinkhole. You're right. This is a crapshoot of places. Or different planets. We have no clue. Do you?" Lochlan said.

"No, but I'll try every sinkhole until I get it right. I'm going back." Solace stood, resolved. She dumped the remains of the liquid in her cup onto the ground, watching as the soil absorbed it greedily.

"Listen," Joe said, his gray eyes burning with passion as he spoke. There was a five o'clock shadow to darken his features making his chestnut hair seem deeper in color. "Every sinkhole *is* a crap shoot. You wouldn't believe the shit we've seen. When we set out, we never once went back home. It's always been in different places we landed. Some are worse than the one we grabbed you from. I'm sure we landed in the same spot three different times in different places. Or we went back in time. I'd like to fucking go ahead in time and find some damned fuel and go home. We may or may not end up on that planet or place of yours again. The one thing I'm certain of is this place is no good. From the type of dinosaurs here, you know the Earth is about to become a mass of volcanic eruption. I for one don't want to be around when that happens."

Solace knew he was right about the planet, or place they were in. Ultimate destruction was at hand the longer they stayed here. The particular dinosaurs gave the era away. Solace had no more clue about where the sinkholes took them than the others. *Crappy crap shoots.*

"How much fuel do you have left?" Solace asked.

"Enough for maybe two more sinkholes. Wherever

we land next better have something or we're up shit creek."

Lochlan laughed. "Look around. We're already in the creek. I can feel the heat of the earth under my ass. From the looks of this era we may be out of time sooner than we expect."

The sun dipped in the horizon. "This time period doesn't have much daylight." Bastian glanced around. "As much as I'd love to stick around and see what happens in this era, it's not a wise idea."

"I'm having trouble with the air," Tain said. "Or maybe it's the smell of the air."

"The volcanoes will start to erupt." Lochlan rose. "We're safer piled together in the plane. First light, we can work on the engines. Daylight is bad enough, but working on anything in the dark is asking for trouble."

Solace silently agreed. She climbed into the plane and settled in a vacant seat as everyone piled inside and the door was closed and barred. Lochlan maneuvered across from the door, sitting on the floor, wide awake taking first shift. Solace was certain this was going to be a long night.

Chapter Three

The clanging of metal woke Solace. As she sat up from her slumped position, Cole climbed into her lap.

"I miss Mences."

"Me too, sweetheart."

Solace ruffled his dark blond hair smiling. Blue joined them. He also missed Menace, the child's deep blue eyes were filled with sadness. His shock of red hair was in disarray. He wrapped little arms around her neck and she hugged him back. She hadn't failed these children, and this was her only consolation. She did need to get back, but now she knew the children were safer with her no matter where they landed.

"You stole me."

The stilted outraged words were from Nick. Solace gazed at him. "We hoped to save your life. I had hoped this plane would take us back to our Earth. You need a doctor. You're injured."

"Many times injured," he snapped back and held out his crooked arms to her. He pointed to his many scars on his scantily-clad body. "Many times heal, me heal me."

"You were exposed in the open. We were afraid you would be killed."

"I go back."

"I hope so," Solace said, her tone quiet.

Nick glared daggers at her until she narrowed her

gaze onto him refusing to back down. The sixteen year old harbored a hate of Doom to his core. At six years, he watched his older brother being left in the forest for the time of the sacrifice. Nick was slashed by a Neandersauri that also broke his arm while he was trying to aid his brother, and was left where he fell. The hybrids didn't want children, and he never saw his brother again.

The teen was a survivor, and Solace knew he went on to help other children. He saved the girl Kiki and her young brother Luke who were now with Doom and Clarity—Solace hoped. Solace wondered if she would ever find out what happened. Until then, the wild child Nick was hers to deal with. His irregular speech was clipped from being nonverbal for years. Kiki taught him or reminded him of his language. Solace couldn't imagine the lonely life of a battered broken child unaided on a dangerous planet for so many years. A thought occurred to her.

"How many children have you lost in your care, Nick?" She remembered Kiki telling her the children of the alternate Earth didn't fare well on Menace's planet. Those children were meek, quiet, and un-disputing, lambs with no backbone. Or perhaps it wasn't a lack of a backbone but more trusting in everyone and everything. Nothing on their sweet unsuspecting planet prepared them for fight. Whereas children from Solace's Earth like Kiki, Luke, Nina, Em, and the twins were fighters, thinkers, and tiny rebels. They could learn to defend themselves and had.

"Not my fault. Not lead to slaughter."

"No, not your fault, but I bet you blame their loss on Doom."

"Some childs want adults, not Nick."

Ah, I see. "So some children saw the villagers and felt they would be safer with Doom?"

"I warn. Not listen."

"Some of the children found their way to him anyway."

"Not all." He appeared uncomfortable.

"You refused to take them to Doom, didn't you? They were killed along the way."

"Better dead than with Doom. I not lead to slaughter. You not get it."

Angrily Nick turned his head to look out a window. She breathed a sigh of relief not wanting an argument because she did get what he said, and the guilt he was feeling showed in his body language. She then quickly glanced back when he spoke, his surprise apparent.

"Not see that before."

Solace shifted the twins to crouch at another window. A gorgonopsid was watching the front of the plane. It was so close she fell back against a seat. Nick hadn't seen the one the day before, only partaken of its victim's meat. Struggling to her feet she saw Bastian and Lochlan at the engine. The dinosaur was fast, and it stood at a man's height with two feet of skull. The twelve-centimeter saber fangs were glistening. Tufts of fur flittered around its body as the dinosaur weaved back and forth. A huge glob of drool slid to the ground from the side of its mouth. Breakfast was on its mind.

Solace banged on the window to get the men's attention then pointed. Lochlan saluted her with his gun. Shaking her head she moved to a seat and faced Nick. There came a rapid series of shots. The earth bumped under them. Nick clamped his hands to his ears until the loud bursts stopped.

"Bombs in guns?" he asked.

"Sort of. You listen to me. This Earth is in its beginning dinosaur stage. Soon the volcanos will erupt. If you take off and run away and aren't here when we leave, you *will* be left behind. So suck it up, soldier. If you want to see your world again, stay put."

"I not leave. I go back for Doom."

"The hybrids killed your brother. Doom was as trapped as you are. He's not trapped anymore. The weapons Clarity has armed Doom and his villagers with make your bow and arrows look like child's play. You'd do better to join their ranks."

"No join. No one help me."

"No you didn't need help, but you've had a taste of companionship. I saw you. I saw you run to help Kiki. I saw you pick up the sword and try and swing. You care. You kept them alive; you saved them. Why not let someone save you?"

"Arms not work right for sword."

"Arms not work right for a sword made for a two-hundred-pound-plus man. The village men and women are huge. Even my sword was smaller. So was Kiki's and Luke's, but they still slice through a hybrid like warm butter. Clarity can make you a sword that will fit you. Doom can teach you to use it." She gave him a wry look. "Unless you plan to use it on Doom. You'll have a problem then."

He raised his chin in defiance. "I not afraid Doom."

Solace chuckled. "Doom won't hurt you. Clarity might stick a bomb up your ass."

"So would me," Blue said. There was a scowl on his face when he stood inches from them, fists balled.

Cole was soon beside his brother followed by Em and Nina.

"There is enough out there to kill us. We need to stick together, all humans," Nina said while the others nodded.

Looks like the tides have changed, Peter Pan.

Nick crossed his arms over his chest and closed his eyes. Bastian and Lochlan entered the plane with Joe and Joey. Tain was last, and he slammed the door closed as the other dinosaurs crept nearer. They were curious beasts. They might have noted the little strange animals could kill the bigger meaner dinosaurs. The scutosaurus were a little too close for comfort, and one nudged the plane. The dinosaur ran its face over the sleek aluminum metal, inching its body closer. Strange noises accompanied the actions.

"Is that dinosaur crooning?" Solace asked.

"Crap," Lochlan said. "If that dino has the hots for the plane and makes his move, we're all—screwed."

"Literally," Solace said, eyes wide.

Joe jumped into the pilot's seat and started the engines which scattered the herd. All breathed a sigh of relief when the roar of the plane caught and held. The airplane jerked. The ground dipped sending shock waves through the passengers.

"What happened?" Lochlan yelled to be heard over the noise the herd of dinosaurs was making.

"It's the planet," Joe bellowed. "This era is coming to an end. A fiery one."

The children began screaming as the ground rumbled and the earth split as a volcano rose in the far distance. Three of the scutosaurus vanished over the side into the mass of lava. A horrific cloud of ash mushroomed into the air.

Everyone jumped into a seat or squished into one. The plane turned from the volcano and started slow, gathering speed. A dinosaur bumped into the side of the plane jostling everyone. Chaos on the ground made it difficult to maneuver to the skies. A scutosaurus went down, trampled. The plane was heading right for it, boxed in.

"Flight would be good," Lochlan yelled, his voice an octave short of panic.

"Working on it." Joe gritted his teeth.

"Really big dinosaur in our path," Bastian said.

"I didn't think it was a speed bump," Joe yelled back.

"Um," Solace piped up.

"Up would be good," Tain shouted.

The plane jumped and rose by inches, higher, higher, until the wheels rolled, airborne, across the downed dinosaur. Solace released the breath she was holding. They were headed up, leaving the mounting pandemonium below. More volcanoes split the earth, vapors rose as ash accumulated. Soon they wouldn't be able to see as a deep blackness formed. The volcanoes would set forth a change in the earth beneath them to last for tens of thousands of years. Solace watched as the surreal moment swept over her.

"We need a hole *now*," Bastian yelled.

"Well, I'll make one magically appear," Lochlan shouted.

"If you're gonna use magic do it now," Joe bellowed.

"I thought I brought up the discussion we don't have magic, no one listens to me," Bastian grouched.

"There," Tain yelled. "The dark hole, it's not ash, its ebony and sleek."

The darkness appeared from nowhere. Joe turned the plane sideways and slipped into the hole. They escaped as the world beneath went up in flames and the dinosaurs continued to die in volcanic ash.

Chapter Four

"I have to go after her." Menace was pacing the main room. Others watched; the children were sleeping.

The day played over in his mind. The war, the plane, Solace. They lost some of their villagers but thankfully not many. Other villagers suffered much more. It was clear from the fallen the hybrids lost the fight, but their clash wasn't over. The hybrids now knew what to expect, surprise was no longer on the villagers' side. The ground ran in rivers of red from the blood in the field and forest. The trudge home was weary, and all were exhausted. Kiki cried herself to sleep while Luke lay on the furs wide-eyed until ever so slowly he closed his eyes with his tiny T-rex friend stroking his forehead.

They were inside the main hall. Food was spread out, barely touched. Fermented drinks flowed but not in celebration; it was to calm frazzled nerves. With Solace and the children gone, there wasn't much reason to take part in victory. Menace could see the faces in his mind of the little twins. Thankfully, Solace was with them. Did she think the plane would take them back to her Earth? Nick was injured and Solace explained doctors on her planet could heal his arms. She hadn't wanted to leave—she smiled at him, was heading toward him. She must have thought the children would be safe.

"It's been a long hard battle, Menace," Doom said.

"Wash, eat and sleep, and in that order, my friend. We will talk soon. We all know now that the hybrids have seen flight. Something inside them mixed with the human DNA we sacrificed might stir a memory, or already has. We all saw the hybrids champing at the bit to get to the strange machine. It's imperative we fight harder. Clarity is almost positive the plane won't be back. The hybrids must not have any type of flight. Solace isn't dead."

"She's lost to me," Menace said. Her life may as well be as elusive as death.

Menace stopped pacing to gaze at Doom and the others. All were weary, and the children lay haphazard across the floor on furs. Kiki lay cuddled up to her massive hyena Bongo, her brother Luke, and his tiny T-rex. The dog, Bubble-gum mourned the loss of Flight, his favorite child while Muffin, the female cave bear-dire wolf-wolverine hybrid groaned and settled near the children. Many of the village children were gone, and though missed by all, everyone felt the loss of Solace harder—except one. Flight's mother sobbed in her husband's arms. Edge shed no tears for the son they'd had for less than a year. The boy always knew his real father would come for him. Menace was as astounded as the others but deep down not surprised. The idea gave him a tiny flicker of hope. Clarity could be wrong. There was a chance the plane might come back.

Menace went to his room and took the steps up to the high outside door two at a time. The scent of blood was heavy on the breeze. The cold air on his bare chest raised goosebumps. It was the ice in his tortured heart that chilled him to the bone. He ran to the cave where the hot springs waited. He tugged at his leather belt dropping it to the floor where it clattered. The tools on the belt were better than he ever hoped to own. Steel blades, not stone or bone. Knives that could slice with little thrust. Weapons Clarity introduced to them all. His hide pants were next to drop to his ankles, then hide boots, and he stepped out of them and into the sunken roundish depth of a water-filled hole, up to his chest.

The hot, spring-fed pools were numerous. Many families or couples could bathe together at the same time. Menace was alone. The rocks beneath him lit when touched by flesh. The florescent light aided him finding the soap they used in the wooden containers. He washed at his flesh, ridding it of blood and muck. He dunked under to submerge wanting, wishing, to scrub the day's events from his thoughts. Menace gasped when he came up for air. Underneath the rippling water were the same tattoos he always wore on his flesh. The same damning images of his betrayal to humans while he tried to save his lost village. The tattoos were for nothing. His people were long dead, and their loving remains gone but not forgotten. He had no one to protect when he was the lone survivor, and yet, he wasn't ready to hand over his life. Something inside of him knew there was a bigger purpose.

Nothing mattered except Solace. Bowing his head into his hands he damned himself for not running faster. Solace explained what a plane was but to see something larger than any bird on his planet fly and devour live humans was indescribable. Clarity said the people within weren't injured or eaten. Every strange thing Solace said to Menace enveloped his mind.

If a plane came through, why not the weapons Solace said were guns? There must be more to the sinkholes than first thought. Were they being manipulated by a higher force? Soon his head was pounding.

He sat soaking, watching the moon through the foot-high gap on top of the draped leather partition. The position of the white planet called a moon rose higher. Was Solace on that moon? She claimed it didn't have life. Solace claimed there were many planets in her universe and more were being found. How could Menace's planet not be in Solace's universe? She was mystified and mentioned the sinkholes might be gateways to portals. She could be anywhere or any-*when*, in time.

Nightmare scenarios plagued Menace until Doom joined him. Menace was dragged from his thoughts. Together they sat silently watching the same stars through the cracks in the hides protecting the pools from drafts. The three bulwarks outside, the same as Muffin—two male another female—would warn them of any intruders. It was highly unlikely any hybrid lurked, they were off licking their wounds, regrouping. The mass killing field where bodies lay would keep the other predators busy. In the distance was heard the roaring of many meat eaters. No remains would be found come morning. The blood would be licked clean. There was no doubt more would soon be spilled.

Menace gazed at Doom, noting he was submerged as was Menace to his shoulders. There was something different about Doom he hadn't noticed. His burden appeared lighter. Something had changed. Then it struck Menace. From Doom's shoulders to his neck, his skin was without any blemish. Doom was shirtless in their dwelling, and Menace was amazed he'd not seen the phenomenon. Was he so overwhelmed with his own loss he saw nothing else? The idea woke him to reality.

"Where are your tattoos?"

Doom sat higher and with a thoughtful expression rubbed a hand over an unblemished chest. "I think I died on the battlefield today. Clarity said there are aliens who created twenty Earths, all in different places of growth, all with a changed situation. She says an alien is a different being. Perhaps these have a little more knowledge. I'm not sure how to describe what an alien is. Clarity explained the name is given to someone not of your own place, a foreigner, but this one was from another planet or galaxy. I'm still trying to wrap my head around what she told me.

"She met with one of the aliens. It appears she had an interesting time of it. The alien healed me and took those I thought I wronged with him to their new destiny. The marks you bear are not your own. We are not to blame. They are deaths, not your fault."

"Then why do I still have them?"

"I don't know. Clarity saved me. She thinks I may have needed to be dead to connect the other souls with their new destiny. She fought with the alien to a degree and demanded I be returned to her. The aliens are having a difficult time placing people where they need to be. She thinks they are manipulating the sinkholes but not all. There are beings out there who are far more dangerous than the one Clarity encountered. That is why the hybrids must never have space flight."

"Will these aliens talk to me?" Menace's heart beat faster.

"I don't know. Clarity thinks they're gone. Or at least will no longer interfere with the changes in our world. They sent the first human by accident, or maybe Alice came by accident, then the aliens continued to send others to keep our extinction at the proper rate. Clarity said we were meant to die and leave the hybrids this planet, but something went wrong. The aliens cannot allow the hybrids to win.

"With the coming of humans, our world changed the hybrids, and now us. The hybrids want space flight, but they can't have it. If they are given the knowledge of flight, entire universes will be at risk. Clarity must be protected at all costs; she has within her the designs of spacecrafts. The monster that took the children and Solace is called a plane. Clarity hopes the plane will return to her Earth. She says if it does, then Solace has a chance to find the sinkhole that brought her here before. But she isn't certain. We need to continue to wage war until every last hybrid is annihilated."

"I need my Solace back."

"I know, because I can't live without Clarity."

"Finding Solace is the most important thing I need to do."

"My friend I don't know how to open a sinkhole. Neither does Clarity. If a chance arises for you to leave, take it, but for now we need you."

Doom stood and grabbed a hide towel. Menace did the same. Doom had brought clean deer hide pants for Menace. The ones he shed were covered in blood as well as his foot coverings. They dried, dressed, and barefoot, walked back to the hall where the others slept. Menace dropped his soiled clothing. They needed a good washing. Clarity sat at the head table with food for Menace. He slumped in a chair and absently broke pieces of bannock to push past his lips. He chewed mechanically, looking around the large expanse of the main hall. His gaze then fixed onto Clarity.

"Tell me about the aliens."

"They seem to be some kind of overseers for twenty Earth worlds. The planets were spread out on a screen of sorts in a projection. They moved around the walls. They were all different sizes and not all were round. I don't know if we are all in the same universe or galaxy. One planet was dead, and one will be soon. Each planet is in a different stage of development. Some are filled with varying DNA. I was told your people were set for extinction, but the hybrids were never supposed to have space flight or the capabilities they possess. When their intelligence began to improve rapidly, the overseers became concerned. Your Earth is in possession of all the materials mine is. If the hybrids succeed, they will join with other aliens in other universes. All worlds will suffer. It's now hybrids that need to become extinct."

"Why doesn't the alien wipe them out?"

"I think its balance. It's why you and before Doom and a few others carry the tattoos. The aliens take the DNA of the dead and send them to other planets to form. Their introduction has to be slow and the planet must be prepared. You can't take a group of people and introduce them to a new world when you haven't prepared for them. It would be cruel. If there are others on the planet, those already there shouldn't expect a strain on them. It causes intolerance, fear. The alien overseers are learning from mistakes. Look at my world. When the new humans appeared on Earth, the Neanderthals went extinct. I'm not defending the alien's actions; I'm trying to understand. They aren't responsible for all of the sinkholes."

Clarity gazed into his eyes and her sorrow reflected his. Solace was her friend. She was missed by everyone not just Menace. Dropping his bread, Menace took her hands into his. Like Doom, Menace had been born a leader, color blind and ambidextrous. The features were how the people knew who must lead.

"If I call out to these aliens will they hear me?" he asked.

"I'm not sure. I was microchipped because of them. They removed the chip once Doom was healed. Solace is from my Earth, and the alien was interested in her. She might be in their radar. I hope in my heart they mean her no harm and will protect her until you can be reunited."

"We are still at war. We need you, Menace," Doom said.

"I will fight, but after I *must* find her."

"I'm certain you will," Clarity said.

Clarity squeezed his hands and rose from the table. She went to lie down on a large fur, Doom joined her. The floor was littered with sleeping bodies. Menace sat alone at the table. For a while, everyone would remain together for safety. Menace picked up his food knowing he would need his strength in the days to come. Everything was tasteless, it was as though his senses were disconnected. He was right; love came in every form and left a void when those you loved left. Solace left with his heart, his flesh, his soul. Though a fire burned not feet from him it was no wonder he was still chilled and upon his arms remained the goosebumps.

****

Outside the homes, the villagers gathered. The

bulwarks patrolled the area. The beasts stood at little lower than Menace's shoulder height on all fours with Muffin the smallest. The name Muffin was given to the huge beast by Clarity. Menace thought back to when he first heard Doom speak the animal's name in a derisive tone. Menace had almost smiled. The idea of him smiling, because he never felt the need before, was such a surprise he had fallen for Clarity. It was soon apparent she had eyes only for Doom, but she and her ideas opened his heart for Solace. For that he would be grateful, he just needed to find Solace.

Clarity said the beasts like Muffin resembled furry tanks, then went on to explain what a tank was. Menace could only dream of being a warrior on her Earth. The weapons she described would kill the hybrids in droves. Guns that shoot a single bullet could drop a hybrid if aimed at the heart or head. The concept made his mouth water with the power Solace's people had. He wondered why the aliens didn't send these weapons through the sinkholes. Unless they feared the hybrids would intercept. Clarity mentioned balance. Perhaps the new weapons the villagers possessed tipped the scales.

"I have no doubt the hybrids are planning a counter attack," Doom shouted. "This would have been the time of the sacrifices with each village taking a day until all humans were handed over. No more. Never again. We have seen the hybrids can't handle the huge number of humans unless they appear daily in smaller groups. We must be relentless. Yesterday was our victory, don't let today be theirs. They will be on the defensive. We must remain diligent in our efforts, and every day after until every last one of them has fallen. It's time we took this planet back."

The villagers raised their swords high. Their numbers were less, but the hybrids' loss was devastating. Their initial attack was a huge boon in Doom's people's favor. The remaining children stood as ready, as strong. Menace raced to Rex, the tiny T-rex had a sword in his claw and was wildly swinging. Menace took the weapon.

"You fool beast, you'll slice your nose off, or someone else's," Menace said. The T-rex stuck his tongue out at him. Luke snickered and draped an arm around his pet.

"He's just trying to be helpful," Luke said.

"Give him a wooden sword left from Blue or Cole," Kiki said.

Luke shrugged and stuck a wooden sword into the small T-rex claw. The dinosaur swung the fake blade and whacked himself on the nose, repeatedly. Luke bowed his face into his hand while Kiki tried to pry the wooden weapon from Rex's claw.

"Listen up," Doom yelled. "Don't take this lull as safety. The hybrids are out there. Groups of five. Arm your pockets and belts with weapons. Remember where the bombs are, there are many left scattered around."

With only a few young children remaining, Doom and Menace gathered them together and locked them in a main room where they had fresh water, food, and warm bedding. The food was only in case of an emergency. Clarity gave each youngster a drink of a potion she created, hopeful the adults would be back before it wore off. The children slept. They didn't want a repeat of the day prior. The only children to head out with the adults were Kiki and Luke. Both the child and teen had their own special back-up.

A massive hyena walked by Kiki's side along with a tiny T-rex, the large mutt Bubble-gum and the bulwark Muffin. Both children were armed and dangerous. Menace set out ahead. They were hunting hybrids. It was time only one thinking species walked the Earth. It would be human. There was a talk of another mountain where the hybrids were breeding. The village's startling and disturbing revelation was the female hybrids waited for human eggs to impregnate them. Once eaten, human brains gave them ideas, and their victim's stem cell memories.

The mountain was large and the caverns well hidden. Much of the interior was in darkness. Creeping silently, Menace roamed the halls. He held a glowing rock; the warmth of his hand made the object shine. The stone walls dripped in areas. The *kerplunk* of droplets hit the ground, but his feet made no sound. Menace could hear the soft whistling of a hybrid. She was huge when she faced him in a large lit cavern. Eight feet high, broad, muscular, wearing a loincloth around her hips. Her six teats were visible. A hybrid was capable of a multi-birth. Menace knew if a female was born she would be killed unless she possessed a killer instinct with zero empathy. The Neandersauri female was a baby maker of evil filth.

The hybrid screamed at him as he approached, he set his rock down and gripped his sword in two hands. Menace could smell her rage. How dare a simple human come near her greatness? She was queen hybrid. About to be dethroned. She swung a claw in his direction, and he dodged with ease. The blade of his sword struck up high into her chest, through her hard flesh out her back. The hybrid gasped and clawed at her chest when Menace pulled the blade back, her face a flurry of surprise. Humans shouldn't be able to kill a hybrid. Menace grinned evilly.

"Payback's a bitch, *bitch*."

Motion from within her body began and Menace could see the inner Neanderthal trying to rip through her host. The guts ripped open and as with birth the body came forward covered in slimy blood. The female hybrid dropped to the ground dead. The Neanderthal hissed at him, but she remained attached to the dead Neandersauri with three long tubes. Two were for discharge, the other a feeding tube. Menace cut the cord and ran it through.

Doom raced into the cavern and stopped in his tracks. "That is disgusting." Clarity was behind him, a hand to her mouth.

"Four to go," Menace said and clapped Doom on the back.

There was talk of five hybrid females. All lacked sympathy and were chosen to live and carry on breeding. They split up and continued to search. It was imperative any breeding females were dispatched before the hybrids could mate and create more beasts. The young grew to adult size within a year.

Menace killed another female. The female's lack of skill to protect themselves made them especially vulnerable. The hybrids counted on their size and the feeble weapons humans made to keep their reign of terror alive. Menace ran the beast through the belly making certain to kill the Neanderthal within. It became apparent the females hadn't been warned of an assault. None knew of the human's weapons and skill. The hybrids were lazy from being pampered and spoiled with food and no hunting. Waited on since birth they were unaware of their fate. All that was required of them was to give birth. Menace was surprised male hybrids weren't sent to guard them but wondered if any had thought to, or if too many had been killed. Did they protect their own? Did they have any idea they should?

Covered in hybrid blood, tired from the kill, tired from his overwhelming emotions, Menace stumbled to the high cave opening and gazed about. Solace was his only thought. He was elevated up the mountainous hill with a bird's eye view. Below the fighting was strong. Kiki sent an arrow flying felling a velociraptor near Luke. The dinosaurs weren't helping the Neandersauri, they wanted fresh meat. Muffin grabbed the back of a hybrid's neck and crushed it, tossing it into the air. Heath, a human from a different earth world than Solace swung his sword. Controlled anarchy was what Menace was thinking.

He shook himself trying to concentrate on the task at hand, there were more hybrid females to kill. Screams came from within the cave. The hybrid number was diminished but their fight was strong. Menace's was stronger.

"Hear me," Menace bellowed. His fists were balled, his arms raised, his sword held high. Passion exploded from within. His loss was killing him. "I will exterminate you all to reclaim what's mine. You will fall fast at my hand. You will fall sooner than you think. You will pay for what you did to my people, you damned dirty hybrids."

Menace wanted the hybrids dead. He had to figure out a way to find Solace but couldn't until the war was at an end. He was ready to take them all on, today, this second, alone though he knew he was not. He shook with his fury. Two hybrids attacked from behind and, surprised, Menace was knocked from the cliff opening with a hybrid. Arms pin wheeling, clinging to his sword, the ground and death was fast approaching. Menace howled his fury, Solace was his. To die from a fall wasn't his destiny it couldn't be. He was supposed to battle. Doom needed him. He should have been more cautious.

Solace.

"My mate, aliens. Take me to my mate," he bellowed. "I can't end like this after everything I've been through." The ground was only feet away. *"She needs me."*

The ground shuddered and split as both man and hybrid fell into a sinkhole. They were soon separated. Menace slipped along the sides of the hole which became a tunnel of frozen walls. The rapid descent became worse until he was suddenly airborne and free from the shaft. Menace fell like a stone into a snowdrift.

The bitter cold assaulted him. He stood shaking off the snow he could. Wearing only hide pants and boots, no shirt, he was soon shivering. Everywhere he gazed was a fluffy thickness. The sky above was what his friends described as drab gray. He was alone. Normally when the snow was this high he and the other villagers became dormant and hibernated for at least six weeks, it was a necessity to their survival. Menace was wide-awake.

What the hell?

In a pouch he possessed matches and tinder but there was no wood to start a fire and warm his increasingly freezing body. Saved from one death to be thrown into another. The snow was almost to his thighs. He had asked to be taken to Solace. If she was here she needed him. Arms wrapped around his chest he surged forward picturing her cold and alone. The image of her suffering drove him forward. His eyelashes became clogged with snowflakes. The air he breathed was different than on his planet as though too much too fast slipped into his lungs. The puffs he exhaled haloed his face. He trudged on. Amidst the misty haze of flakes was a spiral out of the ordinary flittering toward the sky.

Smoke.

New determination fired his steps. The fluff puffed as his knees rose to spray his belly. Exertion kept the freezing at bay but his stomach and chest grew bright from cold. His growing labored huffs sent spittle flying to freeze mid-air. Distant mounds gave birth to massive trees, trees bigger than anything Menace had encountered. The spirals of waving life reached his nostrils and he consumed warm air. The scent of meat carried. Mammoth.

Menace kicked a trail around the tree, his frustration was increasing. An indentation caught his attention. A door. Using his shoulder he shoved hard until the wood began to give. The warmth from beyond was a driving pull. Harder he strained at a massive wooden structure at least a foot thick. When the door flew open Menace had his sword drawn and fended off an arrow aimed in his direction.

"I thought you were an animal." A strong voice called out. "The night is not fit for man or beast. Come in and close the door."

A man stood, bow in hand. He lowered the bow

maintaining close watch on the stranger. Menace understood a few of his words but not all—enough to know he was in no danger, he closed the heavy door. Menace sheathed his weapon and took in his surroundings. The colossal tree had been hollowed out. Massive tree limbs were high enough to use as tunnels and there were many. Though frozen outside huge leaves bloomed indoors. The housing was warm, many of the people were clad in simple leathers or furs.

"I mean no harm," Menace said. "I am in search of my mate, my female, a woman."

The man holding the bow spoke. "I am sorry, there is no other. These are all my people."

Again Menace understood only a few words, but he understood Solace wasn't among them. Disappointment settled like a stone in his belly. A woman crept forward with a warm fur hide. He draped it over his shoulders. Next came a bowl of steaming broth.

"Come and sit by the fire."

The man gestured as he spoke and Menace hungered for the warmth of the flames. Everyone in the tree house was silent as he moved. A small child whispered to her mother but was hushed.

"But mother," was whispered. "He wears faces on his body. Is he one man or many?"

"I don't know."

"I am one man with the burden of many," Menace responded.

Puzzled the child cocked her head. Menace wondered if she understood. Menace went to sit on an object draped in furs. Another woman rushed forward with a hide for him to place under him, he remembered he was covered in blood. The snow had cleaned his body but not his hide pants. The meaty flavored broth he sipped was delicious. The others gathered closer. From similar openings many more entered. The tree was large enough to support many families in the low rounded trunk that stretched to higher levels. The faces of the young were fascinating. These people kept their own offspring.

"Do dinosaurs walk this planet?" Menace asked.

"I don't know what you mean." The arrow man sat across from him. "I am named Dagger."

The words were similar yet different. Menace caught only a few here and there, but enough to piece everything together.

He pointed to his chest. "Menace."

"A warrior's name."

"Yes."

"Which humanoid do you war with?"

"No humans. Hybrid dinosaurs that kill my people. Do you have other humans?"

"Yes."

"Like you?"

Dagger cocked his head. "Nine."

"You have nine other types of humans?"

Dagger shook his head. "Trois." Menace was confused until Dagger held up three fingers. "Trois, human types."

It occurred to Menace trois meant three to this man. He wondered if nine meant no. He sipped the broth and was given a cup of water. The water was warm and sweet. Within the treehouse were higher sections with balconies. There were a few people draped over the banister watching.

Dagger pointed to Menace's tattoos. "Your

people?"

Menace nodded. Dagger removed his shirt and startled Menace. His body was well muscled and well proportioned. There were odd markings on his body that Menace didn't understand. Not tattoos of specific things as were Menace's, Dagger's were different, small connecting patches across his shoulder blades flowing together as one.

Others were bare-chested and all sported the same markings. Soon the others were grinning. It was simple well-meaning banter to show off differences. Menace was handed a huge chunk of meat dripping with juices. One bite and he knew it was pure mammoth, the taste varied from the mastodon mammoth hybrid his people hunted. Both meats were delicious, but this was a bit juicier.

As he gazed at the people around him he had the odd sensation he was seeing all men. It wasn't long before his intuitive nature came forth and he guessed what he was seeing. People of color had come through the sinkholes to Menace's world. People of all colors were fascinating to the villagers. Gazing at their grins Menace knew he had yet to discover deeper secrets of these first peoples who carried on their flesh everyone, every human color to exist in their future. He wondered why he was sent here. Where was Solace?

Chapter Five

The bright white of the snow hit them covering the plane's vision as they entered another world. Joe battled the horrific storm but Solace could see the frown lines increasing on his furrowed brow. Heavy flakes splattered the windows then turned to hail which bounced with a *ping*. The wind gusting tossed their plane up then down. It was neither daylight nor darkness they witnessed when everything was a pure white nothing.

"I can't see shit," Joe bellowed.

"Look, that might be land," Bastian said pointing.

"Can't tell how deep the snow is," Lochlan yelled.

"Doesn't matter, the stretch is open and I have to bring the plane down, now," Joe yelled. "The wings are icing. One temperature extreme to another is a killer."

Solace watched as the ice began to form on the window in front of her. Snowflakes of dread collected making the clear glass frost before her eyes. Below a solitary flat area was approaching. If it was a covered lake they would be drowned unless frozen solid. Solace's heart hammered. Her teeth rattled with the plane. The wheels made contact, bounced, and slipped as the plane teetered sideways. A wing hit the snow and sent the fluffy white powder flying. Lochlan jumped from his seat to race to the other side of the plane to throw his weight as a counter. The wheels lifted for a moment then settled down with a bounce and teetered. Lochlan raced to the left. The plane jumped and he toppled over for a moment before regaining his footing. He stood then, in the isle, arms outstretched waiting to see if and where he would need to be next.

"Damn it, we're skidding," Joe called.

"Down," Solace shouted.

Lochlan was thrown into her lap as the plane crashed through a mountain of snow obscuring all vision. The plane came to a complete stop while the children cried out. They were in darkness. A flashlight came on followed by another. Glow sticks came next.

"What happened to the lights?" Tain asked. "They always came back on before, after we left the sinkholes."

"Maybe the landing did it," Bastian said.

"I don't know," Joe said.

"Is everyone all right?" Solace shouted. She righted Lochlan who fell into the seat beside her.

Nods from different directions confirmed there were no casualties. Faces looked eerie in the strained glow.

"We're going to have to keep watch. The snow's so high we could be buried," Bastian said as he looked through a back window. "We don't want to asphyxiate."

"It's not really falling, it's more blowing than anything," Joe said as he peered forward.

"Hopefully the snow will be an insulator, it's going to get cold, fast," Solace said. She shivered. None of them was wearing the proper clothes for winter weather.

"Break out the blankets and furs. Solace is right,

it's going to be a cold one." Joe went to his son and settled a few Hot Pockets around him. He did the same with everyone else.

"Snow might be a good sign," Solace said.

"It might take more gas than we have to get this puppy off a runway of deep snow."

Joe sounded tired. He pulled his son into his arms. Em and Nina crept up to Solace who encouraged them and the twins close. Nick hadn't spoken. Solace was used to his silence. The teen didn't speak often or well. His perfected scowl was centered on the window to his right. Solace could see he still hated the world, all worlds it would seem. She placed a blanket near him, it was his choice if he wanted to use it or not. The scantily clad teen glared at her but shivered as he pulled her offering over his body. Solace hoped the plane held more furs. In this cold they would all need extra warmth.

"Darned thing," Blue grumpily said. He reached down, yanked a heated pad from his ass, and placed it on his tummy.

"I'm hungry, Daddy," Joey said.

"We'll break out some provisions in a few hours. Right now we need to rest."

"But we just woke up."

"Daddy's feeling a little tired."

Everyone settled. Solace was worn-out as well. Terror took a lot of energy. Joe pulled his son closer. The combination of body heat, warmers, and blankets coupled with the panic of the flight soon had everyone asleep.

****

"Where do you think we are?" Solace asked.

Flickers of sunlight shone through the windows in the morning light. The children remained huddled together. There was snow as far as the eye could see. Solace didn't think there would be any dinosaurs in this mess. Though she could be wrong, anything could happen. A furry T-rex the size of a house wouldn't surprise her. She groaned as the images of a furry alligator crossed her mind. A hairy brontosaurus was next. She damned her imagination as the image of long golden hair flowing from a velociraptor came next. She pictured it blinking with big blue eyes and puckered red lips. Solace gave herself a shake.

"Don't know," Joe replied. "It'll take some time to dig us out."

"Look." Em pointed in the distance.

"Damn it," Bastian said. "Mammoths. I'm so sick of ancient Earth."

"How ancient is always the question," Tain muttered.

"They must be heading farther north to get away from the snow, if there's mammoths there must be a glacier with a dryer cold air," Lochlan said.

"I thought mammoths liked cold weather," Nina said.

"They don't like to get bogged down. Too much ice and they freeze to the ground. Nothing like getting eaten alive," Lochlan said.

Solace placed a quick hand to her mouth remembering the immobile hybrid and the raptor. That was an image she wouldn't soon forget.

"Maybe we should shoot one in case there's no food around here. If we're going to be here a while we may as well have food. We have some supplies but fresh meat is better. And if it's possible we could use the hide to drape over the plane after we shovel the snow off it."

The others agreed with Joe. The men went to the plane compartments and pulled out furs made into clothing telling Solace they'd landed on another strange planet and killed the beasts for warm clothing. Many more furs and hides spilled to the ground.

"This reminds me of another cold planet maybe fourteen thousand years in the making." Lochlan struggled into a reindeer parka, slipping it over his head. "I wonder if the Neanderthal is still alive here. They weren't on the other planet. We stayed on that earth for a few months. The humans were suspicious of us and kept their distance. I think it was the plane. We couldn't leave it unprotected for any length of time and it took a while to fix."

"Do you think there are hybrids here?" Nina sounded scared to death. She, Em, and the twins huddled together.

"If they are they'll be hibernating," Solace said to soothe the girl and the others. "I doubt much is awake or on the move right now."

"Let's go boys," Joe said.

All four men left the plane. Solace slipped into furs from a pile on the floor. She gazed at the children.

"There's more here to wear if you drape it around you. I could use some help."

Nina was quick to scramble to her. Solace could see the snow was deep. She intended to pack down as much of the white stuff as she could. Lifting her face toward the direction of the shots fired she noted the tiny outline of men compared to the huge shaggy beasts. An inevitable stampede started, minus one mammoth. While she tromped through the snow around the plane she uncovered small sticks and frozen foliage useful to start a fire. The older girls came out to help soon followed by the little ones, Nina helped the twins, Joey, and Em onto the wings to clear them off. A cluster of woods wasn't too far but Solace wanted the children to remain within bullet fire. She knew different earths, at least the ones she'd been in so far, held many undesirable characters.

The four men returned using the hide as a sleigh bringing a load of meat. All were sweating with their effort. The mammoth hide was huge, Solace raced to help drag it with the aid of the other children. With help, they pulled the meat off the hide using the snow-covered ground as a natural refrigerator. Nina, Em, and Joey left with the men to help tramp down more snow and offer aid. Though only five the boy was strong, Joey had his father's will and determination. Solace knew there was something special about the boy. A mini Joe and bright beyond his years.

More meat was unloaded and Blue and Cole stayed behind. The snow was too high for them and though they were small it was easier for the others not to have to drag them back and forth.

"I'm starving," Blue said.

"Me too," Cole piped up.

"I'm starvier," Blue said

"Are not, me is," Cole said.

"I think the term is hungrier, and I can hear both your tummies rumbling," Solace said and chuckled.

With the fire well established, Solace used a few of the sticks they found to skewer pieces of meat and cooked chunks of mammoth. The twins held the sticks over the flames roasting their meal though she noted some meat fell into the fire. It didn't matter, they had a ton of it, or six. Solace smiled at them, in furs they looked like bear cubs. Cole, the quieter of the two, groaned as more meat fell off his stick. Blue helped him. She turned slightly, her smile faltering, and noticed Nick scowling at her from a window. She resisted the urge to wave her middle finger at him. *Dour little puss.*

The men unloaded and went back for more. This time they brought the tusks, one at a time. They hacked what meat they could from the leg bones to use as well for weights. The children were fed by the time the men had gathered what they wanted. Solace had a meal ready for them but they only shoved a few bites into their mouths, there was much to do.

Joe handed Solace a few kerosene lamps. She cut a chunk of fat from the mammoth and set it to boil down for the light they'd need. She didn't realize how much she missed regular light while at Doom's village. She had taken the plane for granted. Oil from an animal could stink.

The trail of blood was becoming obscure as the snow began to fall in earnest. Using the knives, they had as much of the meat and blood scraped from the hide as possible. The two older children and Joey were allowed to help while the twins were given rocks to use. If a few holes were punctured it didn't matter but Solace doubted the boys had the strength to do any damage.

"This is like being home with Clarity and Doom," Nina said wistfully.

"I hope we go back the next time," Em said, the twins nodded.

"You like doing this stuff?" Lochlan said, amazement in his tone. "Don't you wish you were sledding?"

Nina chuckled. "Well we did on the hide."

"Wish we had a snowmobile," Tain said.

"Skis would be nice," Bastian said.

"I want hot chocolate," Joey informed them.

Joe placed a hand onto his son's head. "We do have hot chocolate. I was saving it for you but there's enough to share with the other kids. Even the grouchy older one. That teen's a hot mess."

"He's been through war," Tain said. "You can see it in his eyes. He's a tough little shit."

Solace concurred. Nick was a little shit all right and glaring at all of them from a window. Lochlan waved at him enthusiastically, a smile plastered on his face ear to ear. Nick's eyes widened and then he looked away. Solace chuckled.

"Wish we would land on a planet with doctors," Tain said, though he was smiling as well. "That boy is all twisted up. Maybe that warps his mind too. That and having to stay inside the plane. Do you think he'd run if set free?"

"Nick isn't stupid," Solace said, returning to the task at hand. "He's driven by hate, but he's also filled with worry. Don't let his scowl fool you. Half his family is back on Menace's planet. He is capable of great emotion. Good, bad and the downright ugly."

After the hide was cleaned to the best of their ability, they attacked the snow surrounding the plane to clear as much away as possible. They set up the tusks over the plane the points crossing, and draped the hide over as a shelter while they worked. A few large rocks and mammoth knee and foot bones were used and with the help of the others were rolled over flaps to keep the hide in place. Piles of meat were left to freeze under the mammoth hide close to the plane on one side, a fire burned a few feet away on the other side.

"There's so much meat," Solace said, gazing around.

"That's almost half of the carcass. The rest will freeze tonight on the bones we left," Lochlan said.

Solace looked at her garments and grimaced. "I'm covered in blood."

"We all are," Joe said.

Their skins, clothes, and hands covered in the red substance, they used one of the several cooking pots filled with hot water draped over numerous fires they made to wash. Clothes were scrubbed with snow and set inside the plane to dry. Solace constructed a shower area also under the mammoth hide, free of snow and using a blanket for privacy the adults bathed and changed. The children already fed, the rest of the cooked meal was carried inside. Numerous pieces were placed on a bone platter to share. The twins and Joey picked at leftovers while enjoying the promised hot chocolate. Exhausted the adults all sat drinking coffee inside the plane. Solace could hear Nick slurping from his cup while he sat with wide-eyed wonderment. She felt sorry for him for a brief moment. Did he even remember chocolate?

"Daddy, are we camping?" Joey asked.

His father smiled and ruffled his hair. "It appears so."

"Except for the snow this isn't so bad," Em said.

"I want to go home," Nina said. "I want to see Menace and Doom and Clarity. I miss Kiki and Luke and even Rex."

"Why you get in plane?" Nick demanded.

Nina gazed at him then ducked her head. "You were hurt. Kiki is so good with a sword and needed to stay and help. I'm not as good. I know my parents are dead, they must be. You're my family too, Nick. I didn't want you to be all alone. I was worried you'd be afraid of a doctor, the least I could do was hold your hand."

"Thank you," Nick said. The scowl turned thoughtful.

"We can hold your other hand," Blue piped up and for a second Solace thought there was a hint of a smile on Nick's face—then it was gone.

"What should we do with all the meat out there?" Bastian asked.

"It'll freeze so it should be okay," Tain answered.

"We'll have to keep watch. With the blood and the smell, we might risk carnivores," Bastian said.

"The blizzard may take that fear away for a while. We're going to have to wait out the storm. It's building up again. Then we'll need to make a runway," Lochlan said.

"That's going to be difficult." Solace was thinking. The snow was thigh deep. The men were lucky the guns could shoot from a distance or they never would have gotten the mammoth. Even with all of their combined help it would take weeks to clear enough room for a decent runway and if it continued to snow their efforts could be lost in a single day.

"What else can we do?" Joe said.

"We can get started in the morning. The suns down and it's too dark to see. We need to dry as much of that meat as we can. Even still the weight will be a problem," Lochlan said.

"We don't know if winter has started or if this is Mother Nature's last hurrah," Solace said.

"We'll find out soon enough," Tain said. He flexed his muscles and stretched his neck. He was built powerfully, and as always Solace compared men with Menace. All of the men on board were well built, with Bastian the biggest, but none came close to her Menace.

"If winter is getting started we'll need to make every bite of food count," Solace said.

"We will," Joe said and yawned. "We can hack at the rest of the mammoth tomorrow and bring the rest back here. It'll last us a month at least."

"We'll need more than mammoth," Bastian said. Again Solace marveled at how dark the man was. He was beautiful, and when he smiled, which was often no matter the circumstances, he could take her breath away.

"Menace showed me how to find different foods in the forest in his world, on my own planet I know what's edible. This time period may be different but those trees hold a wealth of sustenance," Solace said. "If this is natures last roar of indignant defiance it means there will be new growth under the snow. I can find it."

"Pft," Nick said and guffawed, his hair fell across his eyes before he tossed his head back. "Blue and Cole can find food. Nina is expert. Em can make meal with root five different ways."

"You taught them well," Solace said.

It was true. Nick spent days going over what was edible with the children on Menace's planet. Nina often praised his skills, as did Kiki. Solace wondered how the others were making out. She missed not only Menace but all of them. Even Heath, the cowboy wannabe who never shot a gun in his life. He was from another Earth and on that planet weapons didn't exist. It was hard for the gentle man to kill anything.

Solace settled down with the children for the night. The mammoth hide made a difference, they weren't as cold. They had placed it fur side down, wanting to freeze the bits of blood and meat still clinging to their hastily acquired tent in case they would have need of the skin for another reason. Solace remembered the men said they spent a few months on a different kind of Earth, they mentioned they'd had need of a shelter like this one. The tent also made the inside that much darker and quieter. The plane rocked less from the winds assault.

Where are we? She wondered as she lay still. Mammoths were ancient creatures, the time period could be anything. The forest in the distance was filled with massive trees. She wondered if the Neanderthal lived here, or others. Another thought occurred, *when* were they? How did time exist on other planets or planes of existence? If they found their way back to Menace's planet would they return before the battle, or farther into the future? A time when Menace and the people no longer existed, or back in time to when the hybrids were only beginning. She wished she could have spoken to Clarity about her concerns, and that thought led her to wonder what had happened to her friend before Solace was taken. Finally her runaway thoughts tired her mind and she slept.

****

When morning came Solace noted Nick glaring out the lone back window they kept uncovered. She cast her gaze around wondering who caught his wrath so early. Everyone else was asleep. There was a shout from outside and the plane was pelted with objects. Solace gasped and bounded from her seat upsetting Lochlan who was in the seat before her. A *thunk* sounded. Everyone was up.

"What the fuck?" Tain bellowed.

"Is it hail?" Bastian shouted.

The twins raced into Solace's arms followed by Em. Nina went to sit with Nick.

"Is furred things," Nick said.

Lochlan glanced out the window pushing the two young teens aside. "It's people," he shouted. "They're throwing spears at us. They must think we're a mammoth. Damned idiots."

He tossed his coat on, and grabbing a gun, he raced outside followed by the other men. A shot was fired and the shouting stopped. The sun was up and Solace could see the stunned expressions on the faces of the people before her as humans filed from what appeared to be the mammoth's belly. Solace joined their ranks. All of the hunters held spears and were covered from head to toe in furs. The gaping people looked ready to bolt. Solace held her empty hands up.

"We mean no harm. We only want you to stop throwing things at us. We have young children inside our, um, tent. Our shelter, home—domicile." She wasn't certain if they could understand her at all.

"We were hunting and saw blood. Our dwellings

are low on fresh meat and this is the first hunt of a new season. We wanted mammoth. The snow was almost gone. Normally a last blizzard blows to trap an animal. We thought you were that animal."

Solace blinked when the man spoke. She understood every word. The man had just communicated a few sentences using words from three different languages.

"There is enough meat here to share. We are peaceful and lost," Solace said. "Are we welcome in your home?"

"You say you are willing to share your kill?"

"Yes," Lochlan said. All nodded. "There's more out there, enough for many to eat for many days."

There was discussion amongst the hunters. It was unclear if they understood him. Lochlan made a sweep with his arm and the unmistakable large bump in the distance caught the newcomer's eyes.

"More meat," Bastian said enunciating his words as if it would help.

The one who first spoke held his hand up. "You are permitted to come with us. There is much meat and it will be welcome. There must be a storm blowing in. There were loud thundering noises."

Solace realized the hunters weren't aware it was the men's guns that made the noise. The weapons were hand held and she doubted the others had seen them. From the grin on Lochlan's face she knew he guessed the same and his weapon was shoved into the belt at his hip.

The meat had frozen overnight and the others used large axes made of stone and wood to cut manageable sizes. The mammoth in the field was picked clean and the rest of the bones hauled back to the plane for transport. The hide was left to protect the plane. The hunters had sleighs they used to transport meat. One was used to pull Nick and the smaller children. Em was scooped into Lochlan's arms. The snow was too high for eight-year-old legs. Nina huddled close to Solace. They followed a path the hunter's had left and Solace stood wide-eyed when a massive group of trees came into their line of vision. Mountainous behemoths, some that reached into the sky, others shorter but sheltered. She was stunned when a door opened. Numerous people greeted the hunters while eyeing the strangers. There was a great deal of chatter and speculation.

"This is wild," Lochlan said.

"If you mean primitive cool I agree," Bastian said in a loud whisper. "Damn this is amazing."

"Daddy when we get home will you build me a tree fort like this?" Joey asked.

"Bud, this would take decades," Joe replied, eyes wide.

Solace couldn't believe her eyes as she stood gapping at her surroundings. The interior of the tree was deep rich colors of brown and hunter green. Children of all ages gawked at them. Blue and Cole hustled off a sleigh to stand beside her. Lochlan settled Em onto her feet. Nina went to kneel close to Nick. The group huddled together. Some of the people didn't appear as friendly and held weapons loosely. Not exactly hostile, some gazes weren't altogether welcoming. Solace didn't blame them, she wasn't certain what to make of the people staring at her. One man in particular seemed to be checking her out. He was huge, almost Menace huge.

The meat disappeared into a side dwelling. The fires that blazed were soon covered with haunches of dripping mammoth. Solace and the others hadn't eaten and she knew, like her, their mouths must be watering. For the size of the wide high dwelling it was warm inside, she was already beginning to perspire. Many fires blazed, many warm furs littered the ground, benches, and high platform beds. Few dividers were set up for privacy. Numerous pieces of wood were carved into animal heads. Totem poles were in various places. Wood carvings were on the numerous massive branches within the dwelling.

"Something smells wonderful." Bastian said.

"I'm so hungry I could eat anything right now," Tain muttered.

Different scents drifted to Solace, not only the smoke of the fires, which escaped from tiny smoke holes, but an ancient earthy scent. The parts of the floor not covered in fur were moss. Edible mushrooms were growing. Looking closer she saw wild onions and chives. There was a greenhouse of food within. Whoever these people were they were brilliant with their design. Higher wood baskets were strategically placed for sun. The green tops of vegetables were visible.

Inside the large dwelling was a man with his back to her. The crowd seemed to part until he filled her line of vision. There was something about the way he stood. Something familiar. He was covered in furs from head to toe. He turned with a slight motion.

"Menace." Solace raced into his arms.

Stunned surprise greeted her as she was scooped up into powerful arms and crushed to a massive chest.

"Solace, my Solace."

"How did you get here?"

"We waged war again yesterday on the hybrids. We killed the five female breeders, at least I hope we did. I wasn't thinking, I was so angry and wanting you so badly. I was attacked from behind. As a hybrid and I fell from the cliff I screamed to the aliens I had to find you," Menace rushed to say. "A sinkhole opened last moment and I fell into a pile of snow and found my way here."

"Aliens?" Lochlan asked.

Menace narrowed his eyes onto the man and stepped forward, fists balled. "You, it was you who took what is mine."

Solace saw a red hue creep over Menace. Lochlan was no wimp, but Solace had seen the same furious gaze cast at Edge once from Menace, and the man had the good sense to back away. So did Lochlan. She gripped Menace harder.

"This man is Lochlan; he thought he was saving me. This is Joe, Joey's father, Flights father, and Bastian and Tain. These men have been traveling through sinkholes from different time periods or something. We don't know what is going on. Do you? What about aliens?"

"Is that guy you said expected you to call him father as big as this guy?" Joe whispered out the side of his mouth to his son.

"No daddy." Joe slouched in relief. "Edge isn't as big but real close. All the men there are big."

"Great," Joe muttered.

Glaring, Menace said, "Clarity was kidnapped during our first confrontation with the hybrids by an alien who claims dominion over twenty Earth planets in different stages of growth. When she explained that to me I was worried Solace was kidnapped by aliens. Are you aliens?" He tightened his fists and took a step toward Bastian.

"No, Menace," Solace interjected as her eyes widened. "They are men from my Earth. I think. At least they are from *an* Earth and I know Joe is from my Earth because Joey is." She realized she had yet to find out about the others, their lives were such a whirlwind of events. "That's Bastian, Tain, Lochlan and the one holding Joey's hand is his father, Joe. Please tell us what Clarity said about aliens."

"The hybrids were never supposed to learn the way they have, or as much as they have, their intelligence was not meant to be and must be stopped before they discover space flight. Showing up in that plane will make them fight harder. You men never should have come to my planet."

Joe stepped forward with Joey now in his arms. "What length would you go to save your son?" he demanded. "What length were you willing to go for Solace?"

Solace watched as Menace relaxed, his fists unclenched. Menace was suddenly surrounded by children demanding his attention. Blue and Cole held their arms up to him but instead he released Solace and dropped to a knee where he could embrace all of them, Nina and Em included. Only Nick remained seated on the sleigh, glaring.

"I see you've maintained your sunny disposition," Menace drawled to the teen.

"He's hurt," Solace said. "We've had a heck of a

ride in the last few days. I'm no doctor." She looked at a man who was studying her, his regal stance made him appear leader. "Do you have a healer here? A doctor who heals wounds, hurts, pain?" She wasn't certain which word he would understand.

"We have a Gift Giver," he replied. "My name is Dagger."

"I'm Solace. Can your Gift Giver help this young man?"

A woman approached and proceeded to pull at Nick's clothes. He shook her off, slapping at her hands. The woman eyed him, cocked her head and left. She tossed her arms up as though she had better things to do and didn't look back.

"That was foolish," Solace snapped at Nick. "She might have been able to help you and we are strangers here. You have lousy manners young man, or should I say *little boy*."

"No touch," he said with a snarl.

"Fine. Lay there on the ground then until you develop some sense." Solace began helping the children shed their furs.

"Come to the fire," Dagger said urging them toward the heat.

A young girl about Em's age began giving out wooden cups of water to the children. Em exclaimed in delight announcing it was sweetened with honey. The young girl approached Nick with hesitance. Solace knew Nick didn't fear children. He stopped glaring long enough to take the cup, drain it, and lie back. He was soon asleep. The Gift Giver returned and offered Solace a sly smile. Dagger picked the boy up and carried him away.

As Dagger left, he informed his guests they were free to look around. With so many eyes on the strangers, Solace knew they were considered no threat. The men carried handguns they kept concealed. Dagger's people wouldn't know what to make of them if they saw the weapons. From the spears standing upright in various places Solace understood these were a primitive people with intelligence. Simply gazing around showed her their ways were inventive. Their home was stunning.

Solace stepped into Menace's arms and they kissed. Other women came forward and took the children to various hearths to feed them and offer changes of clothes. There was great interest in Tain's plaid shirt and a number of young women flocked around the men with interest. Solace took Menace's hand and they walked near the base of the tree. The ground beneath their feet was littered with large furs, with the moss surrounding them on the outside away from the fires. Rows of cordage sectioned off food areas and the children stayed away from the somewhat lush areas.

"The trees base is lined in cement, it seems, or a harder substance," Solace said. "Remarkable. Look at the rich soil where the moss is. They're growing food in here, plants in strategic places where sun filters in but the fires keep the plants warm. Look up there, those aren't mere smoke holes."

Not only the base but half way up was a cement-type substance and it was thick, keeping cold out and warmth in. The rock material helped keep the plants warm as well. There were mammoth furs hung from many of the walls. Solace cocked her head. The amazingly thick tree had been gutted on the inside leaving a number of huge live branches used as walkways, or perhaps they were roots from the surrounding trees. The branches weren't from the tree she stood in. There were holes where the branch entered then looked to head outside to another tree base. Another way for smoke to escape and allow sunlight in. The holes appeared to be the right size for each individual branch. As she watched a man used a large knife to gently scrape away bark to enlarge a hole allowing branch growth.

She could look straight up and see the top of the tree, it was apparent the rest of the tree was left partially intact, the sides tapering smaller, about twenty feet high, but not enough weight strained the base. To strengthen the tree there were layers of cement half way up the base to the dwellings to form a sturdy foundation. She puzzled at the branches that interlocked and when the pair climbed higher she stood stunned mouth agape. Beneath them a number of branches were fitted with support beams.

Tree after solid tree formed to make a circle from what she could see, each with a sturdy supporting base from branches, each housing twenty or more people. She was gazing at an entire community. Perhaps an entire race. Each person had lines, perhaps tattoos, including the smallest of children which led her to believe they were birthmarks. Across their upper chests in fine rows shoulder to shoulder, were rainbows of color in fine lines. The colors of man. Their language was comprised of a number of languages. Solace was well versed in different languages but there were some words she didn't comprehend when overhearing conversation that was no doubt about the visitors. The words were strange and on a deeper level she knew she should know them.

The children of these people were cute, little surfers, of all ages, as they slid down tree branches covered in moss in bare feet. They moved from site to site. Home to home. There were no boundaries. There were no barriers. The surroundings belonged to them. The children swung from vines. Every head of hair fluttered in the breezes they made. Blondes, brunets, gingers, chestnut, black, tawny, and more. Thick hair, thin, long, short, curly, straight, and wavy. A kaleidoscope of humans. The trees were filled with delights of sights and sounds. The children were singing and a few adults joined in. They were a happy people and Solace could tell there was much love within these homes.

"It's not hard to make cement. But this stuff would last a long time. I don't remember any in our Earth history of ancient homes with cement." Solace scratched her head. "This must be a different Earth, not a different time period."

"As long as I've found you I don't care if it was Earth's Hell," Menace said. Their fingers interlocked.

A woman approached Solace and held out reindeer skins. She shuffled her feet, went red, and urged what appeared to be garments onto her. The women then bid her follow. Solace was confused. She glanced up at Menace.

"What you're wearing is frightening to them. You are, um, a bit ripe."

"I stink?" Solace was mortified.

"No not stink," Menace was quick to say. "Then

again you could swim in mammoth dung and I'd still hug the stuffing from you."

"Always the romantic."

Solace followed the woman. She led both Solace and Menace, because Solace wouldn't let him out of her sight, through a heavy hide she pushed back. A tunnel of interlocking cement and wood and bone took her to a large bathing area. A small waterfall was near the back. Soft light from bowls filled with melted fat bathed the interior. Torches were lit. The woman left and Solace stripped, her toes dug into the luxurious furs beneath as she moved. Menace followed. The water was heavenly warm, as she slipped lower from rock to rock.

"Spring fed," Solace said.

"Like home but different."

Solace turned into his embrace. "I missed you."

"Did anyone hurt you? Or anything?"

"No, we've been running for our lives since I left. It's nice to be in your arms. I ached for you to hold me. You make me stronger."

Menace drew her higher into his arms for a kiss. Their tongues met with a leisurely dance. She missed his taste and moaned in delight. When their kiss broke Menace settled his forehead against hers. He placed his hand on her chest.

"My heart is beating again," he whispered. "The frozen pain is gone, you melted my icy agony. A fishing line is what you are to have hooked my soul from the depths of despair. I am alive again. Your kiss filled my quiet lungs with your breath." He pulled her head to his chest. "Listen my love, it beats for you."

"I knew we would be together. There was no other option." She ran her finger down his cheek.

"I would have looked forever."

"Me too."

Menace nuzzled her throat, kissing his way up to her lobe and chin. She may have melted his heart but it was because of the fire he started within her belly. Every inch now burned for him. Her flesh tingled, remembering what his touch would do. Waist deep in incredibly warmed water he explored her. Menace kissed her, lowering to fondle each breast then lave her bellybutton. He nipped first one hip then the other.

As he moved back up her body she shivered in delight, a heady euphoria engulfed her. He claimed a deeper kiss of her mouth, as he lowered a hand to dip in the water. Solace moved against the two fingers that found her heat. She ground against the thumb at her bud.

"Menace I want you," she panted raggedly.

He buried his face into her hair. "You have me. You woke me from living death—again. Our hearts can't be denied. Yours beats with mine. When you left all sweetness turned sour. Let me love you. I live in your heart, remember? I am home again."

Menace eased his cock into her, lifting her. Her legs wrapped around his waist. She devoured his power into her flesh. Each stroke tossed her up into his arms. Menace gripped an ass cheek and the back of her neck. Soon the still water was awash with waves at his motion as he dropped to his knees to keep her in the water's warmth. In his loving embrace Solace wept. A small shudder rocked her. When she peeked up at him a tear fell from his eye followed by another. His tender expression showed his love.

The pounding of his heart boomed against her and

Solace met his pace. She wrapped her arms around his neck and cried out when he thundered his release. When his body slowed he crushed her to him. For a moment they stayed together refusing to give up the intimacy. Menace nipped her throat making her squeal. With tenderness he eased her off him and he wrapped an arm around her shoulders watching the water droplets fall from his hand onto her skin. She wondered what he was thinking.

"My Solace. I wish I had a name you could be proud to call out."

"Menace." He cringed when she spoke. "Menace is a perfect name. Because it belongs to the man I love. Any name you have is perfect."

"Really?" he cocked an eyebrow.

"Yes."

"So if I were named Bubble-gum…"

"Never mind, or I'll be calling you Muffin."

Menace chuckled, the sound filled her being, a gift to lighten her soul. "We need to go back and help Doom."

"Yes, we do," she concurred.

"First let me help you wash."

A creamy soap had been left in small woven baskets for use. Solace washed her hair enjoying the flowery scent. She moaned when Menace let his hands glide over her back to her rounded ass. She turned wanting the feel of his skin on her heated flesh. Fingers she adored soaped her breasts and throat. They were both panting when he rinsed her clean. Menace was hard again; he pressed his cock against her belly.

"I can't help it," he said as though to apologize.

She smiled at him and gripped his swollen member

in her hands. "I missed you, too."

"You must be hungry."

"I am for you."

Menace nudged her legs with a knee and soon he entered her with a quick thrust. The water churned as he took her in a frenzy. Solace gasped from the passion that exploded from him. His grip was almost too tight.

"My Solace," he said panting.

His hands squeezed her body to him lifting her higher in his arms. Menace roared when he came and her release caught her by surprise. She slumped in his embrace; her body was shaking. He kissed her throat, her cheeks, holding onto her as though his life depended on it. He was a powerful man in a strange place and she was his lifeline.

Menace lifted Solace to her feet. "As soon as the snow clears and we can take off, we're out of here, Menace." Solace was gazing up at him. "We will get home."

"In that plane?"

"It's all right. Don't be worried."

"I wasn't worried just wondering. Do we have to take Nick?"

Solace groaned. "I'm afraid so."

"Maybe a mammoth will poop on him and solve our problems."

"Ew. That would be one big pile of crap.

"Exactly."

"Teen years can be hard no matter the situation. You have to admit he has had it rougher than most."

Menace led her from the water where they dried and dressed. Solace took her time running a soft skin across his broad back, loving the feel of him. She moved lower to rub each ass cheek, then lower to his calves. Menace bowed his head. There were the tattoos of his fallen people on his back and legs. Burdens he carried because he had once been a leader. Somehow the fates knew to place this burden where he couldn't see it. Solace was glad of that, there were so many.

Each tattoo she wiped dry with gentleness born of knowledge. When he turned, she stood to stand quietly before him. More images adorned his body but were of the sacrificed victims.

"They are gone in body but are safe with you," Solace said.

"My heart is safe with you so they are doubly protected."

They took a leisurely stroll back to the others. The sky was already growing dark and many of the fires were banked. Wicks were snuffed out, a few torches remained lit. Furs were laid out for the new guests around the main large fire. Menace and the others helped get the children settled for the night. Solace again wondered about time in these ancient worlds. She wondered when the earth of this world would settle into twenty-four hour time periods.

A variety of food was left out for the pair to pick at in the stillness of the evening. The treasures of greens filled her mouth in a flavor dance. A fermented drink quenched her thirst and relaxed Solace. The last few days were beyond hectic and filled with fear. Solace's fear was gone. Wrapped in Menace's arms she fell asleep.

C.L. Scholey

Chapter Six

Morning was a bustle of activity. The women were preparing breakfast and Solace watched them take turns stirring up different foods. In a huge, thick, worked hide hanging over hot coals was a mixture the women added black beans to, as well as garlic and powders smelling of chili, chipotle, guajillo, and salt. Another woman smiled at Solace and encouraged her to watch as in another hide was placed masa harina, salt, and water. They took turns with a wooden paddle beating the dough. The dough was transferred to husks. The villagers grew corn which amazed Solace and they smoothed the dough over husks to form a thin layer. The filling was added and soon the tamales were steaming.

A coarse bread was made for the pesto. A paste of pecorino, salt, various seasonings, oil and white wine vinegar was shaped into a ball. Solace could feel a frown curve her brows. She pointed at the cheese to a woman who smiled. On Menace's planet they had cow-like seal water sea creatures that came on land to give birth. In exchange for protection, the seal-cows, full of milk, were approached with watertight baskets and milked. The creamy substance was turned into delicious cheeses and butter. Solace wondered if these people had the same creatures. Though it was doubtful; the beasts on Menace's earth were hybrids. The woman led her to

84

a smallish door, the top half opened. Within were mouflon with their young. The mouflon had been domesticated by these people, and Solace noted many of their young resembled sheep.

A few children sat or played, the older lambs bounced or playfully butted one another. The room was lit with many bowls filled with beeswax and wicks on high shelves where the mouflon couldn't reach even if standing on hind legs.

After a glance Solace could see no fodder, the floor was a deep rich, dark dirt and well cleaned. "What do the animals eat?"

"We collect the tall grass for them. The grass is stored in a different room. They are fed during the daylight hours and once at night with a single candle in the hands of ten feeders. As the grass is dropped, each light is extinguished so there is no chance of a fire. We must be very careful with fire."

No doubt.

"How long have you been breeding them?" Solace asked. The ground was soft under her feet. The cement was as high in the paddock at the walls as it was in the living quarters. Solace supposed it wouldn't be good for the mouflon to eat the tree base.

"Many generations. I have very old bedding from long ago, the wool on the beasts is getting softer in time from the beasts hair. In spring after shearing, the mothers will be allowed loose during the day to mate but will return at night to the safety and warmth of the tree. We allow no rams in here and hunters have killed many who try to take the herd from us. When the lambs are born there is a huge feast of the males delivered. The meat is so tender and juicy. The mouflon who must

give up their male babes are pampered and will
continue to give us much needed milk for cheese and
butter."

"That's remarkable."

"Their manure is especially good to fertilize our
many gardens and because we keep them all year we
have an endless supply. Our gardens are well tended.
They keep us healthy. Before the lights are all out," the
woman continued. "Each child takes a cup and fills it
with warm milk. Though the milk is mainly for the
children, cheese and butter, a few adults have been
known to find pleasure in the drink with spices added."

Solace loved warm milk with cinnamon on cold
sleepless nights. She wondered if these people made
eggnog. Solace was led back to the fire with food where
she sat between Menace and Lochlan. She dipped her
coarse bread into the pesto. It was delicious. The bread
was sweetened with honey. The children drank cups of
warm milk. The visitors were informed they had two
main meals, early morning, then late evening with
something small during the day if needed. Yellowish
wild carrot, and white and purple carrots, white turnip
stored were dished out from a stew that sat cooking at
night. Cucumbers cut and pickled were offered. Next
came thick slices of mammoth.

Some of the older people rocked on wooden
rockers, padded, near the fires. Little ones gathered at
their feet for stories before beginning their day.
Beautiful wooden stumps were carved and polished into
animal heads. A number of cradles were scattered at
various hearths. Each family gathered to take a share of
the meal at the largest fire, and though there were a
number of fires they were smaller and used for teas.

"How long before the snow is gone?" Joe asked Dagger.

It was apparent to Solace, Dagger only understood a few words. She tried to explain using the various forms of language the people spoke. Solace had traveled all over her Earth, and her army background with picking up languages fast was a boon. Dagger nodded to show he understood much of what she said.

"Your words are different and same," Dagger said.

"Your words remind me of many languages where I come from," she informed him.

"Other clans, not close speak some of our words but not many. They are different from us."

"I think the ones you speak of we would call Neanderthals. Stocky, shorter well built with large brows? Adapted to colder weather."

"Yes. Them and another. Like us but not, darker skin, tall. Our kind have traded with them. We exchange food but they want mates. Different cultures but good hunters. They need to be to cover their skin from cold. They live in caves. Primitive but a good shelter from the snow. A few have tried to make shelters of skins but the snow can be very high. Some do not make it through the cold."

Solace's mind was in high gear. She wondered if these people were *all* humans, all color, race shape and form. Mixing with another humanoid to form complex humans, today's humans on her Earth. Though she knew she wasn't on her early Earth, if what Menace said was true about the aliens, the plane didn't time travel through sinkholes, it was world to world travel. *What a strange concept.*

"My friends and I want to know if the snow will

melt soon," she asked.

"Yes."

"In how many days?"

"What is days?"

"Days. How many can you count? Yesterday was a day. Today is now until dark, then the sun will come up, then tomorrow starts a new day, how many tomorrows or todays until the snow goes?"

"No count, not with sun sleeps. Everything must sleep, I sleep, the world does not exist for one sleep to be more important than the others on this planet, or off this planet. We could say when the moon wakes, but I don't care when it wakes or when the sun sleeps, they always do. Weather is far more important to me and my people. We need to know when to hunt and what animals will be coming through the vast plains near our homes. The weather tells us this. The first small cold and the deeper cold has come, then the next small cold, the cooler warming and then the hot and so on. There is no today, tomorrow, or yesterday. I don't understand what that is."

"You count in seasons," Solace said. "Great," she muttered.

"Solace if we are back as far as fifty thousand years, time is different. These people could be twenty-five, or fifty or one hundred with the rate of the way days change so fast. And who knows who they are," Lochlan said.

"So how the hell do we find out when the snow will melt?" Joe asked.

"I guess when it melts," Solace said.

That was met with several groans.

"You need to fix the lights on the plane and

anything else broken in the last landing," she said.

"True," Joe said.

"We need to get out of here," Bastian said with a hissing snarl. "I like the attention of women as much as the next guy but these females are freaky."

Solace grinned at him. Bastian was probably the darkest human these people had ever seen. His skin, a solid beautiful ebony, appeared to be a magnet. The children stared at him, the women too. The men didn't seem to know what to make of him. Solace didn't know what to make of the people. Interesting didn't cover her emotions. She gazed at them like they ogled Bastian. The man was handsome, well built and every female was eager to touch him.

The tree people's light body color and patterns weren't unusual but still stare worthy. As was their different hair colors, or highlights. Solace wondered if some had chosen to mate with the Neanderthal and the new humans and left. Spreading out over the continents. If they had would their children be born one color, and hair with the same colors and with some highlights? Forming her people. Some with brown eyes, green eyes and blue eyes. Gray eyes from a few people stared back at her. Were they a lost race even on her Earth?

If others set out, Solace knew the terrain would help define skin tone and facial features. The Neanderthal nose was wide to help warm the air before entering their lungs. The shapes of eyes would differ over time and continents.

"When will your sun come to warm you?" Solace changed tactics.

"We are rain when we cry and the sky above opens, fire when food is needed, wind when we must hunt. When enough of us feel the same, the elements change. I do not understand tomorrow. But the sun shines most days," Dagger said to add to her confusion.

Solace gazed at Dagger, she turned to Menace. "Each word is in a different language. I've traveled all over the world and understand him but it may take a while to place each word without offending. Plus there are some I don't know. Every race incorporates their own everyday language. Some of what he speaks is slang."

"Tell him we need to leave when the snow is gone," Joe said.

"Snow gone soon," Dagger said. "Then we hunt. We will be the wind."

"What do you hunt?" Menace asked.

"Megaceros."

Solace nodded. Many hides littering the floors were large and she guessed it was the giant deer Dagger mentioned. There were also mammoth skins and hides, but they seemed to define separate living quarters and to be used as doors. The large outer wood door to the treehouse remained shut to keep in the warm air. A thick hide was draped in front to aid with insulation. Tendrils of smoke wafted higher then slid out manmade cut slits. She noted many small hides were shifted aside to allow more smoke to filter when the fires blazed larger and hotter during the day. The sunlight aided in lighting the domiciles. The tree homes were a fortress, well protected from man or beast.

Groups of families began to break up and begin separate duties. Wanting to help, Solace went to a group of women. She was welcomed with greetings and smiles. The women were boiling the roots of a hickory tree until all the water evaporated, leaving black salt crystals. Others were making teas of chamomile, linden, and lemon balm. Vervain was added to another cup and taken to Nick by the same little girl. He drank it down then settled back.

One woman held up a bowl and explained later she would give it to the sad boy. Hawthorn berries to help with his grief. Solace was certain the Gift Giver was helping Nick. The stubborn teen would only accept drinks and food from the girl-child but Solace was certain Nick knew who was aiding him. A compromise, Solace supposed. The Gift Giver didn't seem to mind. The little girl stroked Nick's face, Solace wondered if she was checking for heat but the child was interested in his twisted arms.

Nick allowed the girl to study him and told her the story of his breaks. She sat back to listen, entranced. The Gift Giver gazed at Solace who motioned to his arms. The Gift Giver shook her head in a negative way. She couldn't help. Solace didn't think so. At least the teen was engaging with the girl, trying to speak though his words remained clipped. Clipped wings, clipped words. Solace felt a moment's pity until Nick caught her glance and glared at her. He wanted no pity. He was a proud man-child.

Solace searched for Menace and saw him with other men around the huge main fire. Dagger and some others were discussing a hunt. Dagger was gesturing with a weapon, a gutting tool that resembled a Wyoming knife. Dagger's was made of a bone-rounded handle. The hook looked to be flint. Menace was beyond interested. Besides making love, the man had a passion for hunting. Solace was more interested in the food the women were making. She sent a passionate gaze in Menace's direction. Another woman tittered and they all turned back to the mammoth stew that would be served at their evening meal.

****

Menace listened to Dagger describing hunting and gutting. He itched to get his hands on the tool he was using. Normally when Menace slit a kill he placed his finger on the inside to slice-guide his knife carefully through the hide and he did it fast on his planet. The scent of blood drew many carnivores. He wasn't certain what animal they were going to hunt but he wanted to participate. The tool Dagger held was undeniably sharp on the inside curled end of the hook and dull on the outside. The tool made perfect sense. Menace memorized every part of it, aching to go home and craft his own.

Dagger examined the sword Menace had brought with him through the sinkhole. The metal was foreign to the man and he was as curious about the weapon as Menace was with the knife.

"This was made?" Dagger asked.

"Yes, on my planet. A female named Clarity showed us how," Menace replied. "It can slice through the tough hides of the hybrids and into the Neandersauri within."

"You will bring on hunt?" Dagger asked.

"Of course."

Speaking of the upcoming hunt returned everyone's attention back to the main task. To include the others, Dagger was using exaggerated hand signals to describe their prey. Menace thought it might be some kind of massive deer. His mouth watered. He loved his planet, but the hybrid dinosaurs weren't nearly as tasty as the food he was served here. Even the mammoth was different, juicy, and tender. Not that it wasn't at home, the meat had a wonderful texture, but this people's way of cooking and what they cooked was flavorful in a different way. Most every village on his planet cooked the same way with subtle variations. When Clarity and then Solace came, the villagers were introduced to other foods. The children adored something called pizza and fries. Solace made ketchup and Menace still wasn't certain of his thoughts on the blood-like-looking substance.

Menace was surprised when sometime later Solace handed him a platter of food. The juicy dripping meat was tucked inside flatbread, and it teased his nostrils. A few reconstituted vegetables were in a broth of soup sitting in a wooden bowl on the platter. He was given a smaller, dull-to-the-touch, eating knife made from bone fitted to a wooden handle; an everyday cutlery.

"I thought a large meal was for the end of the day," he said.

"Apparently this is the smallest meal of the day." Solace settled beside him.

Menace smiled at her and soon noted the treehouse was suspiciously quiet. He noted Dagger watching him. Menace and Solace seemed to be the only ones eating. Solace soon became aware she was the subject of attention and he saw her frown.

"Is it your custom females bring males food?" Dagger asked.

"Only sometimes. If we're not busy or if like today, you have been absorbed with thoughts on how to provide more food we all eat," Solace replied.

"Interesting." Dagger eyed some of his own women. "I would like to hear more."

Menace wondered if she'd made a social blunder. It appeared by her expression she thought the same as some women were gazing with disapproval. Under her breath, she muttered: "The other women gave me odd looks when I made two plates of food. I wondered if they thought I intended to eat both platters. Now some of the older women are gazing at me in annoyance."

"Just tell them you love me so much you can't bear the thought of me hungry," was his amused response.

"You're no help," she grumbled.

"Dagger is waiting."

"We are taught when young to fend for ourselves. I have noticed you wait on the children the same way. Are they incapable of finding a dish and scooping out food when hungry?" Dagger asked.

From her expression, Menace knew Solace understood most of his words, Menace wasn't as certain, it was the amusement in Dagger's tone that spoke volumes.

"Ours is more courtesy than custom," she explained loud enough for all to hear. "The children are in a new place and do not know what is or is not allowed. Or socially acceptable. By bringing Menace, my man, food it indicates to my other friends they are welcome to eat now. We would not be so discourteous as to take what is yours until we are offered from those who worked hard in both gathering, hunting and preparation. We are, after all, guests. It would be rude to make such a social blunder after the women have worked so hard in creating this lovely repast."

There was a collective sigh of relief from the

women who appeared to be holding their breath. Her explanation was satisfactory. Solace wasn't subservient because of her sex—just more courteous. It was the females who were now looking at their men with amusement.

Dagger rose to get himself a meal followed by the others. Solace encouraged the children to do the same. Though Cole and Blue had some difficulty with knives they picked apart the meat, scowled at the veggies and slurped the broth as well as dunking the bread into the juices.

"I wish these people had chocolate milk," Em said.

"I mixed my milk with a little honey, it was good. So was the honeycomb," Nina said as she settled near Menace. He was glad the young girl came to him instead of Lochlan. The child seemed to have a crush on the man. Lochlan didn't notice or pretended not to. Menace didn't want the sensitive young girl's heart broken.

"Can we go home now?" Joey asked his father.

"As soon as the snow melts we are going hunting to repay the kindness of these people. Then we'll see what we can do," Joe replied.

"We shared a mammoth. How much do they think we eat?" the boy grumbled.

"I think Solace's friend, Menace, could polish off a mammoth in a week," Lochlan said, smiled, and winked at the boy.

"True enough," Tain said.

"Maybe but he doesn't eat as much as Doom or Edge," Joey said.

"Edge is the man who was your dad on Doom's planet?" Joe asked.

"Yeah, and he smacked my bum, and I told him you would fly your plane up his ass."

Bastian roared with laughter. "He's your boy all right."

Joe chuckled. "Remind me if ever I meet him to tell him he's not allowed to hit my boy."

His self-righteous tone made Menace scowl.

"It was for your son's own good." Menace wasn't at all impressed. "My planet is dangerous. A willful child could be eaten, if he does not listen. Your son was wanted and loved, by us all." He didn't mention Edge could kick this man all around the planet without breaking a sweat.

"Not love. Fattened for slaughter." Nick was up, and using careful strides seated himself at the fire near Dagger as he sat with food.

"There is a war going on where we came from," Solace interjected. "My friend Clarity has taught the people of the planet to defend themselves." She then turned to Nick. "Perhaps you should ask Dagger if you would be welcome here. You obviously hate Doom's planet."

"Kiki and Luke my friends."

"They chose to stay with Doom and Clarity," Solace reminded him.

"They stole them."

"Do you really believe that?" Menace asked. "They have been taught to more than survive. There is no more sacrifice. They can defend themselves with real weapons."

"What is sacrifice?" Dagger asked.

Menace took a deep breath and let his hand trail over his many tattoos. "Long ago, a hybrid was born and then another, and yet more. They destroyed every humanoid lifeform on my planet except for a few hundred of us. They gathered knowledge from humans who came to us from other worlds via sinkholes. This is where the earth opens and swallows people whole. The hybrids wanted the humans that came after the first was found. Her name was Alice, and she saved us and doomed us. The hybrids absorbed the knowledge of other humans who came to my planet, and took their DNA to make their own kind smarter. We need to go back and finish the fight we started, we killed their leader DaV-nin and now there is confusion among the hybrids. If we don't destroy the hybrids, your planet will suffer as well as many more."

"How?" Dagger asked.

"If the hybrids gain space flight they will join with others more evil and kill every planet they land on," Menace said. "You will all end up sacrifices and eaten."

There was anxious shuffling as many spoke in loud whispers. Fear was building and Menace was sorry for it. He wanted them to be prepared.

"I'm sorry I frightened your people. This isn't their fight, it's ours," Menace said. "We intend on winning."

"Then we better get you back to your planet," Dagger said.

"After the hunt," Menace replied.

"Yes, after the last big snow, the weather for the first hunt is favorable," Dagger said. "But explain to me flight. What is a plun?"

"It's a plane," Blue said and crossed his eyes making his twin giggle.

"Blue, don't be rude," Nina admonished.

"He not rude," Nick said. "He four."

"Still rude," Em said and rolled her eyes.

"All right enough," Menace said, his narrowed gaze spoke volumes and the youngsters quieted.

The children were collected to feed the goats while the adults talked. Nick was given another sedative and a warm place to sleep. The Gift Giver shook her head at Menace when he motioned toward him as Nick was lifted to a sleeping space.

"He seems a bit better," Menace said.

"Much anger. Much hate. Mostly the boy hates himself. His wounds will heal. But he may always war within," the Gift Giver said.

Menace didn't care as long as the boy wouldn't war with Doom. The guilt that hounded his friend was palpable. Menace knew Doom would never raise a hand to Nick, even if it meant to save his own life. When they returned he would have to keep a close eye on the boy. Perhaps the Gift Giver could be talked into giving Menace her sedative recipe. Nick was a lot nicer when he was sleeping. The idea made him grin.

Chapter Seven

Looking outside, the season seemed to have changed overnight. Hunter green buds were formed where barren branches once hung. The grass around the tree base was thick and lush. A fresh spring breeze tickled noses. The sound of a babbling brook caught Solace's ears. Excitement was heavy in the air as loved ones were kissed goodbye, safe return was called out. Leather satchels were handed to those leaving, filled with a quick meal and water skin.

The hunters left, both men and women eager to be off. Solace stayed behind to keep the children from following. The day was too beautiful to pass up and all were outside enjoying the end of their long, confined winter. They collected winter cress and day lilies. Burdock stems were only recently budding but they dug for the roots as the snow was quick to melt in the sun. The plants had begun to grow but nature snuck up on them for a last hurrah from winter. A small amount of garlic mustard leaf was found and goutweed. The evening would be filled with feasting. The next day they would need to fix the plane. The travelers needed to leave and hoped with high spirits they would find a planet with fuel. Or perhaps the next one they landed on would be their new home forever. At least, that was what Joe and friends hoped for. Solace and Menace needed to go back.

"I'm taking the twins in for their nap," Nina said.

"We're too old to nap," Blue said, but he yawned.

"It's the air here, honey." Solace crouched down to the twin's level. "I think it's more pure than home. I'll be along soon and may just curl up beside you. I'm feeling kinda lazy today."

The boys groaned but Nina bribed them with honeyed milk and the promise of a berry pudding that was cooking when they left to go out. The women said they would cook the berries to thicken them and pour cream over them with drizzled honey. Solace smiled as they sulked away taking an annoyed Joey with them. Em encouraged him along telling him she would play with him. Solace ventured farther into the wooded area.

A dismal cave caught Solace's eye as she gathered foliage. Her basket full, she wandered over to peer in and placed the basket down. The hair on her neck rose and goosebumps dotted her skin. A smell lingered that made her skin crawl. She began to enter and noted the farther she went the black charring was heavier. The scent was one she couldn't place, but didn't like. Another woman came to her and hurriedly caught her hand, dragging her from the cave. The woman, the Gift Giver shook her head no.

"The dead go in. Only ash left." Solace was told. "The mountain demands our lifeless. The earth shivers and we know when to place the dead inside." Shading her eyes Solace could see a volcano in the distance where the woman pointed. She wondered if this cave was attached. She made a mental note to ask Dagger. Was their resting place an incinerator? She hadn't noticed any grave markers outside, or signs of deceased inside the treehouse.

The Gift Giver smiled at her and Solace offered a tentative smile back. She was grateful the woman said the cave demanded the lifeless; not the living. The women strolled back to the tree home and Solace gave in to her weariness and curled up with the twins for a quick nap, certain it was the air making her tired.

Later, the hunters returned with the remains of four megaceros. Antlers spanning twelve feet, Solace realized she'd seen the antlers around the dwelling but shaped into platters and shovels. The hunting party was strangely quiet. A few of Dagger's people were pale and jittery. Lochlan, Joe, Tain and Bastian held back.

"What happened?" she asked Menace.

"Lochlan and the others in your party made big sounding booms by pointing their hands and three of the beasts dropped from magic. One second they were upright, the next they fell from a distance as they ran. No spears thrown. The sound commanded their death, of the ones pointed to," Menace said.

"Big booming—wait, they shot off their guns," Solace said, relieved. "They did have weapons. They weren't visible if you didn't know what you were looking at. At first, these people thought it was thunder."

"Dagger and the others went after two beasts, but now have five. Though they shared a kill with those you would call Neanderthal. The leader is uncertain if he should be excited or frightened," Menace explained. Solace thought Menace seemed a bit unnerved.

"I explained to you what a gun is," Solace said.

"Explaining isn't the same as witnessing the result."

True. If Menace knew what a gun was and was

uncertain, she could only imagine how Dagger and the others were feeling.

The people were due an explanation. She asked Joe for his handgun, explaining the situation, and then went to Dagger, pulling him aside. It would be a shame if they wasted the meat of such proud beasts. Three of the five carcasses remained outside.

"The boom you heard were from weapons my people call guns. This in my hand is a gun." She held it out, extending her arm. "The men didn't point a finger and have a beast fall from magic. This is a powerful weapon. We have tried to explain that we are from a different planet than you in a different stage of growth. There was no trickery used to kill those animals. It's called technology. I'm certain some of your weapons are a mystery to the other humans here. An advancement when they don't understand and might think you have used something enchanted. Don't deny your people this gift from us, please."

Menace had come with her and she knew he was curious about the guns. Solace had explained them to him but she guessed he didn't really believe their power. Now he did. Menace loved a good weapon. Now that his initial fear had swayed to curiosity, she could see he was aching all over to get his hands on it.

"Your ways are different, and yes, the small broad-shaped humans are curious to trade for our weapons. Their spears are thick and must be used in close proximity to a beast. We have shown them how to make spears sharper and able to fly with a hard throw. When they first saw our spears, they were in awe, almost afraid to touch one. The meat is welcome, we will accept it," Dagger said. Solace let out a breath.

"What were those others we shared some of the meat with?" Menace asked.

"A different breed of human. The powerful body, the heavy brow ridge," Dagger said.

"We would call them Neanderthals," Solace said.

"But on my planet the Neandersauri is evil," Menace said.

"We do not find them evil, strange perhaps, but they are a people who are heading off in different directions. Some of the meat we gave them was for travel. If they leave the land there are more hunting grounds for us so it is little we offer in exchange. We wish them well on their journey. They are one in few to look for a different land," Dagger said.

"Will you move away, too?" Solace asked.

"This is my home," Dagger said. "Some say the great waters are rising, but I say no."

"What great waters?" Solace asked.

"The ones where there are huge fish, many the length of over a dozen men. Fish with huge teeth. Turtles so large we could swim riding their backs. The waters have been the same for so long. There will be no change."

Solace wondered if the ocean was advancing. The polar caps froze and melted with seasons. If the melt was getting longer the tree people might find themselves under water in a few thousand years. Certainly not in Dagger's life time but sad. Were these people now a relic in her Earth's waters? So much of Earth's oceans were unexplored. She gazed around at her new friends then pondered their disappearance and demise. Her heart suddenly hurt.

The people in the dwelling were beginning a meal;

some began drying the meat. Menace asked Dagger if he would help him make a knife like he used for field dressing a megaceros. Solace watched them walk off. She gazed around at the busy people noting the children were put to work. Solace hurried to help, then remembered she'd left her basket of vegetation near the cave and left to retrieve it.

The basket was untouched where she left it. She stooped to pick it up and noticed she was being watched. Solace sucked in a breath. Before her was a Neanderthal. He was her height, barrel-chested and robust. His shoulder length hair was thick and dark. She expected him to be dirty but he was clean and washed, his clothing, though not stylish, were cared for. His eyes were dark brown.

"You really are magnificent," she whispered.

He pointed to his ample chest and struck it with a fist. "Gar."

Solace made a fist but only placed it on her chest near her heart. "Solace."

He cocked his head. "Solce."

"Close enough." She smiled.

Looking at the powerful male, she realized why this type of body worked well with the Neandersauri. The exposed body parts she saw were hairy. Gar was an exceptional specimen and she wondered if he were leader of his clan. When he motioned for her to follow him, she was startled but she shook her head no. He growled and snorted, a command followed. She must have hurt his pride. He took a step toward her, and Solace reached for the gun she had yet to give back to Joe. She wouldn't shoot him, but she could shoot into the air and scare the piss out of him.

Solace cried out when her basket dropped as she was pushed aside. She wasn't knocked off her feet, and she retained her hold on the weapon. A female Neanderthal was growling and motioning at the male. She spoke a few words, and if Solace didn't know better she might have guessed the female was swearing at him. The male went red. Solace refrained from outright laughter. The female was verbally kicking the male's ass. *You go, girl.*

When the female turned she railed a few words at her and motioned for Solace to pick up her basket and leave. Solace did, fast. Gar may or may not be leader after all. The female was scary as shit, and Solace took off giving in to laughter.

****

Everything possible they could toss was left behind to lighten their load on the plane. The lights were again operational. The engine was functioning. There was little fuel that worried them all. Their next sinkhole would be their last until gas was found. All were eager to leave even though these were a kind people. Joe wanted advancement if for no other sake than for his son. These people were too primitive in his opinion, though he voiced his thoughts in a kind, well-meaning way.

Dagger said the mammoth hide was still useful, as it was partially frozen, and accepted it as a gift. Solace asked Dagger to reconsider moving his people or at least look to higher ground in a few years. He smiled and said no. Here was where his people belonged. Solace wondered if one day the volcano would blow leading to astronomical occurrences. A tidal wave or tsunami would make short work of their tree homes.

Famine. Plague. Where did these people go? Were their type ever on her Earth? If so, what happened to them? The speculation was endless.

With the addition of Menace, the take-off would be more difficult. But the absence of fuel lightened the load. The people offered dried meat in exchange for the fresh megaceros the men shot. The hunt was considered favorable when Dagger explained the men's weapons. Everyone filed out into the sun to see them off. Dagger's people watched with amazed horror as the engine caught. The noise startled them to flee back. Some ran away. The plane maneuvered forward on the bumpy field that was void of large growth and had dried in the blowing winds.

"Look," Nina shouted.

High in the sky a dark void began to appear. Joe was battling the controls. They needed to sail over the clump of short trees in the distance. When the plane flew into the air heading for the black sinkhole Solace and the others gazed down. From what they saw this earth was still joined to another continent, separated by a massive glacier. Tiny dots walked across the ice and she wondered if it was the Neanderthal. She saw a herd of mammoth being hunted by another group of furred upright people. The plane continued to rise ever higher until everything below became a spec.

"All of what those people built will be deep in the ocean in a hundred thousand years. No wonder there's no trace of them. This clan was older than we thought," Lochlan said.

"It's no wonder there is no record of these people," Solace said in agreement. "Dagger told me their burial rituals. Human remains would be zero because they used a small cavern fed by a gas line to cremate their dead. Leaving no trace for anyone to find, you can't get DNA from ashes. Their ashes were scattered to the wind to be returned to the earth over the snow season. During non-snow the bodies are thrown into a volcano with all their belongings. That's why there's no record of these humans. Even if the trees disappeared under water the cement left would look like coral and blend in. What a shame our Earth will never know them."

"Our Earth will probably never know much of anything if the hybrids aren't stopped if what Menace says is true," Bastian said.

"Hold on to each other," Joe called.

As they slipped into the black sinkhole the darkness gave way to a frigid cold and silence. The lights went out. Solace could see no one and she shivered. She was grateful for the warm hand on her shoulder and snuggled deeper into Menace's chest.

"Solace?" Menace asked.

"Yes."

"Does my planet look like the one we left from above?"

She felt his small quiver and realized how hard this was on him. Menace had never before flown. She knew he was brave, then she realized how brave. Before Joe and the others came he had never seen a plane, now he was in one going where only time would tell. He'd boarded without hesitation. Had she been as brave her first time flying? When she already knew what a plane was?

"Your continents are all attached but from the height of a plane you can't see everything. I can only speculate on what I've seen."

"You mean there's more to the land we saw? That sheet of ice?"

"Yes. If we were in space it would be easier to compare the different planets. But even on my Earth we'd yet to detect a planet exactly like ours. We might have if the sinkholes hadn't become too much."

"Daddy." Solace heard a small voice. "Will we ever go home?"

"Joey, home is wherever you are," Joe said.

"Hang on," Tain shouted.

The plane began to rumble. Menace clutched her harder. When they exploded into a new atmosphere, a few screamed. The sky was blue and clear, and the sudden light made them squint. The plane tilted sideways until Joe leveled it off. The engine sputtered.

"We're out of fuel—hang on," Lochlan shouted.

"We'll crash," Nina cried out.

"No crash," Nick said and pulled her close.

The plane bumped and jostled in the wind then as it skimmed over a large pond it touched down. Solace thought her teeth rattled. She began to loath flight. Menace gripped her harder. The pounding of his heart near her ear was the only indication he was afraid, but she knew the fear was for her. The ground zipped by until Joe brought the plane to a stop. They were alive. Bruised from being tossed but for the most part unharmed. They checked the children for any hurts. Nick scowled when Solace reached him.

"Are you or Nina hurt?" she asked.

"We fine."

Nina disengaged herself from Nick's arms and peered out a window. "Not a mammoth or dinosaur in sight. I recognize those types of trees from my old home and look over there, daisies. Willow trees, oak trees, wild flowers."

"Are we on our Earth?" Em asked with excitement. The twins gathered near her. They gazed curiously, nothing more. They were young when they fell through the sinkhole, and Solace knew they didn't remember their parents.

Bastian reloaded their weapons. Tain grabbed a large machine gun to Solace's surprise. He gave her a cheeky grin as he handed the others weapons. Tain glanced hard at Menace before offering him a gun. Solace took it instead. The small hand gun was shoved into the back of her leather belt. She was afraid Menace would shoot himself.

"Stay close," Joe advised as he opened the door.

Their first tentative steps embarked another journey of discovery. They roamed the lush earth with foliage familiar to Solace. She saw coniferous and deciduous trees with leaves fluttering in a breeze, acorns on oaks, the green husks of the black walnuts hanging full, and berries on bushes. At first she was delighted, as were Em and Nina. Everything was familiar except there were no homes or buildings. Solace frowned. What was missing? Squirrels, birds. There were no signs of life. All was eerily quiet. The sound of their feet on the hard ground was an intrusion. The scents were high of vegetation and raw earth smells. The taste of the air wasn't primal it was—scarred.

"Where do you think we are?" Solace asked in general to the group. "Or *when* do you think we are?"

"No clue," Lochlan said. "It's so quiet."

"The vegetation looks like our Earth, our time, but

there doesn't seem to be anyone," Joe said. "The silence is almost deafening. No machines, no voices, no animals, no nothing. No planes overhead. Not a train in sight."

"Could a hypercane have caused this?" Tain asked.

"No, even vegetation would be destroyed," Solace said.

"Even still there's some speculation of our Earth about a hypercane when the meteor hit," Joe said. "We recovered, maybe only plant life did on this Earth."

"There doesn't seem to be anything here. Maybe we're in an uninhabited area," Bastian said. "Or restricted."

"If it was restricted there would be signs of damage, wouldn't there?" Tain said. "There would be signs period, with some kind of writing or symbol."

"Not necessarily," Solace said and swallowed hard. "This could be quarantined. The signs outside a designated area."

"Spooky," Nina said, in a hushed whisper.

"One person says zombies and I'll shoot you," Lochlan threatened.

"Not, um, the word you said," Solace began. "Disease maybe. There should be signs, a fence, a wall, red tape, banners. If this is or was restricted it has been for a long time. I didn't see anything when we flew in."

They continued on as a group staying close. There were no bird songs or rabbits nibbling the green grass. Not a dog barked. The ground was void of snakes, toads, there were no tree frogs. No helicopters or kites. No engine revved, not one car squealed. A splash of out of the ordinary color caught Solace's attention. She moved closer toward the brush with all trailing. With

110

help the foliage was cut and with a gasp Solace pulled out a little plastic ride in car under debris.

"Plastic," Solace muttered.

"What?" Bastian asked.

Solace turned to the group. "Metal will rust after time, people, everything can decay after an apocalypse, but if not touched by fire, the plastic will last. If that's what happened, this Earth might have died at least four hundred years ago. The amount of foliage, the decay…"

"You can't simply know that," Tain said.

"I'm searching for a plausible scenario. Look around," she insisted. "My dad was a huge post-apocalyptic fan. He and I watched all scenarios. If this is what I think it is we are in danger from animals who are no longer domesticated. Only the biggest and strongest survived. Human life is gone."

"Then we're stuck here forever." Joe grabbed the little car and smashed it to the ground, obliterating it to a mangled mess.

"Not necessarily. We could find the remains of a gas station," Lochlan said.

"Gas station?" Menace asked.

"A substance we need to fly the plane," Solace explained. "A tanker maybe, they have thicker bladders in case of seepage into the oceans."

Menace went to examine the broken toy car. His features became puzzled. "Humans drive in these cars? I'd never get my leg in."

Joe laughed. "It's a toy for a child."

"Oh, I miss riding in mine," Joey piped up. "Why did you have to go and smash it, Daddy?" He and the twins leveled accusing gazes onto Joe.

"Sorry bud, there's no time to play right now," Joe

said.

"Look." Blue inched closer into the bushes. He grabbed the remains of a child's white and red plastic rotary phone and handed it to Menace. Solace chuckled when he stared at it baffled. She leaned in close to whisper to him.

"Put it to your ear and say hello."

Menace gripped the base, put it upside down near his ear, and said hello. Both twins doubled over with laughter. Menace shot her a questioning look.

"Good try," Solace said with a smile. Then to Joe: "Maybe the kids should go back to the plane."

Her suggestion was met with immediate resistance, from the children.

"Not child," Nick said with a glare.

"Not helpful either," Menace retorted in the same stilted voice.

Nick leaned down and picked up a large club of wood. He took a practice swing. "Nina, Em stay close."

They all remained close. Solace stopped and kicked at the ground under her feet. She crouched and looked at Joe.

"Pavement. Maybe a road."

Lochlan heaved a huge sigh. "If you look close enough to those vines you can see the concrete under it. Rubble for sure. Solace appears to be right. Do those apocalyptic movies say why this might happen?"

"Many reasons. War, weather, or people may have disappeared one day," she replied.

"The Rapture?" Tain said.

"If it was the Rapture I'd have family and friends here," Bastian said rolling his eyes.

"The Rapture would have been followed by years

of plagues and war," Solace said. "Everyone would be dead eventually. To me it looks like maybe all life vanished, and the planet went wild."

A low growl made them all tense. From the bushes appeared a massive German shepherd crossed with another large breed of dog or wolf. Solace swallowed hard and slowly went for her gun. The dog looked to weigh three hundred pounds or more, his shoulder was higher than her waist.

"That is one big fucking dog," Lochlan said deadpan.

They spun in a slow circle to keep the children between them and the dogs, as three other massive mongrels, flanking them, joined the beast. Twigs snapped under insanely large paws. Solace heard the loud expelled breath of Nick as he tightened his hold on the club, the whites of his knuckles prominent. Saliva dripped from a dog's mouth. Fangs exposed, the dogs moved forward as one.

"Nice doggies?" Em said on a quiet breath.

"Doubtful," Nina whispered.

Tain shifted his machine gun, and let out a blast. Nick's eyes rounded with surprise as the dog's bodies jumped and twitched until they lay quiet. Blood pooled beneath them. Tain winked at Nick who glanced at his club, huffed in embarrassed disgust, and tossed it to the ground.

"If this is a road, we should follow it," Joe said.

"Keep your eyes open," Solace said though realized mentioning to be cautious to be redundant.

Cole found his way into her arms. Menace picked up Blue; Joe held his son. They kept the remaining children flanked in a circle between everyone as they continued on.

The sun beating down grew hotter. They used the skins of water they brought sparingly. As they picked their way through the shrubbery of obstacles, Solace gathered grapes and apples. Some they ate on the way. When the remains of a battered car came into view, Solace took many of her treats to the vehicle and placed them inside, telling the others the car's heat would dry them out for them and they could retrieve them on the way back.

"If we don't find fuel, what will we do?" Lochlan asked.

"What about hemp?" Solace said.

"We'd need a warehouse wouldn't we, to make enough?" Tain asked.

"We could build a work area. There's enough around to use to make a solid structure. If we can't find a gas tank," Solace said. Then she mumbled, "It would take a while to get enough. Wish Clarity and her big brain were here."

"If plastic doesn't deteriorate, does gas evaporate?" Bastian asked.

"I guess we'll find out soon enough," Tain said.

"Solace is right that tankers have bladders," Joe said. "If one has been beached, we might be able to reach it. I don't know. Can you think of anything else that would cause this earth to be this way, Solace? Nuclear explosions? I'm trying to wrap my head around the idea there is no one left. Maybe there is? What if they were stolen by aliens? Your friend was—even if it was for a short time."

Joe sounded a bit hysterical. She knew he was worried for his son.

"Maybe people simply disappeared for a good reason, anything is possible. Clarity might know more, but that won't help us now. Should we walk half a day then walk back to the plane to spend the night and try a different direction in the morning?" Solace asked.

A yes and a no followed. Then an argument about the pros and cons of continuing. Safety concerns came into the picture. If they weren't traveling with children, the decision would be easier. They debated traveling together as opposed to groups, the season, hazards besides wild dogs. The hours passed as they continued to argue periodically while trudging onward. There wasn't anyone. Tensions rose higher as their walk produced not a soul.

"Solace do you think there are any humans left?" Joe asked.

"Everything is up for speculation. They could be invisible for all we know and waving their hands in front of us. There might be some underground, maybe, perhaps. If we find them, what do we do? They're as trapped as we are."

"They might have fuel," Joe said.

"They might be completely different to adapt to being underground, too," Solace said.

"You mean strange creatures with weird hair and eyes," Tain said and gave her a cocky glance.

"No, I don't think genetically humans would turn into monsters, but they may have had to adapt their eyes for underground light. The sun may be too bright, and their skin could be highly sensitive. It's feasible they may have had to modify certain things."

"Vampires," Bastian said snapping his teeth.

"Vampires, word is familiar," Nick said with a

furrow of brows.

"I doubt they've become blood suckers," Solace said with an eye roll. "What I do mean is I'm guessing they adapted to underground and are staying there where they've known safety. Who knows what diseases we could be carrying and spreading as we travel to each planet?"

"That's something I hadn't thought of," Bastian said. "Then again, I had no idea we were going planet to planet, not time travel or different planes of existence."

"If we've been inoculated can we spread disease?" Joe asked.

"I'm guessing yes. Or our clothes. Look at how the white man gave the Natives small pox through blankets," Solace said.

"Speculation," Tain snapped.

Solace blinked. "Perhaps, but now isn't the time for a war of political words."

"Do you get the impression we're being watched?" Lochlan said.

"Every damned planet," Tain said.

Menace stopped, and grabbed Solace's hand. He pointed. "There."

"I don't see anything," Lochlan said with a frown.

Solace knew Menace could see things others could not. She had come to learn because of his sight he saw different shapes outlined missed by someone who saw color in a different light. The gift was a boon on his planet.

"Trust me, if he sees something, it's there," Solace said. "Ever see a copperhead disappear into its surroundings?"

They all peered toward the bush. A massive winged creature came flying at them with a screech. Nina screamed and shots were fired. The creature dropped near their feet. They crept closer. Solace cocked her head. The bird was an emu, with long wings capable of flight, a shorter neck and legs, and a beak filled with large sharp teeth.

"Hmm, omnivore, you think?" Bastian asked nudging it with his foot.

"I'm thinking food," Joe said and smiled. "Anyone else hungry?"

They built a large fire and roasted pieces of the bird with long sticks. Solace settled back against Menace. She guessed any animal smelling fire would stay far away. The bird was tasty and filling, the skin crispy, the meat tender.

"We should take enough of that bird back for dinner," Bastian said. There were nods of agreement.

"So your world has hybrid dinosaurs that are trying to kill off mankind?" Joe said gazing at Menace while he chewed.

"Yes," Menace answered.

"You only wanted to go back to find Menace, Solace. You've found each other. I wanted my boy, and have found him. We need to stop and settle down sometime. This Earth might be the opportunity we want," Joe said. "The animals are different but not outlandish. The air is good. We aren't in the past. We could assess the surroundings after a time."

"I need to go home," Menace said. "If you chose to stay on my planet you will be welcome and there are other humans. Here is lonely."

"You can kick Edge's ass, Daddy," Joey said with

such seriousness Solace hid a smile. She wondered if Joe had any idea how huge Edge was. Then struggled to keep a grin from view when Joe gave a quick glance to Menace who was scowling she noted.

"We do not fight each other when there is much fighting already," Menace scolded. "Edge and his women were good to you, boy. They fed and clothed you, gave you a home and allowed you to keep Bubble-gum many nights."

"You have gum there?" Tain asked.

"Clarity named the male dog she found Bubble-gum. There are also hybrid cave bear and dire wolf mixes. I think they're part wolverine too. Joey is only a little boy, Menace. Adults in his world are supposed to take care of him, that's nothing new. He wanted his father. You know what it's like to be separated from someone you love," Solace said.

Menace was nodding his head. Blue climbed into his lap and nestled against his chest.

"I missed you."

"Me too," piped up his twin.

Menace ruffled Blue's red hair, a contrast to his brother's light blond. Solace had missed Menace and her heart melted when he smiled. They finished their meal and began their search anew after packing meat into leather knapsacks.

Chapter Eight

Menace kept Solace close. She carried a tired Cole in her arms while he held Blue. They were returning to the plane having found nothing. Em was dragging and Menace crouched so she could ride his shoulders. Joe carried his son and the other men held their intriguing weapons. Menace itched to learn how to use one. One by one they shuffled onto the plane, a refuge of relief.

Solace took the bird meat and other vegetation they found to cook over the fire or in hot coals. They were in need of a meal. Menace cracked nuts with rocks. Solace skewered the meat. She set the men up to dig a hole, telling them she'd line it with rocks, build a fire inside, and cook the rest of the meat in a ground oven for breakfast. Solace claimed her father taught her. Menace was grateful of her knowledge; this planet didn't look like his. The vegetation was different to the degree he was uncomfortable. If this was what Solace was used to, it was a wonder she wanted to return to his planet.

Before long the enticing smell of food brought the children to their feet and they shuffled from the plane to sit around the roaring fire. Solace set the food on a platter of mammoth bone they had brought and everyone took a share. She retrieved the fruits from the car on the way back and set them out to dry further. Menace knew she was planning ahead in case they either remained on this planet or needed dry food if they found gas.

"What does gas look like?" Menace asked.

"Gas is a liquid and you can tell what it is by its smell," Tain said.

"This could be futile to try and find gas. The tanks could be dry and cracked, tree roots may have punctured through, or it may have simply evaporated. What we need is a map or an aerial view," Joe said settling onto a log seat with his son on his lap.

"What about underground gas lines?" Bastian asked.

"The plane is equipped with dual fuel, but how do we find one?" Joe asked. "If we did how do we dig deep enough? Let's face it; we are going to be here for a long time."

"I will find a way back to my own planet and I'm taking Solace and the children with me," Menace said looking at each person. "We are winning the war."

"You seem to have forgotten the kids came of their own free will," Tain said.

"I not." Nick was outraged.

"There was a battle raging all around us," Solace said. "I thought anywhere would be safer for the children. I told you guys before I thought you would take us back to our own Earth. Now aliens are involved. If Menace says our home is the best place for all of us I will follow him. Since you want free will you can ask each person what they prefer."

Slowly the children began to group around Menace and Solace, with the exception of Joey who clung to his father. Joe ran a hand over his face.

"Joe," Lochlan said. "If there are no people here what will we do? Who will Joey play with if the others find a way back to their planet? Things are so screwed up we may not need the plane. A sinkhole could open up anywhere at any time. I can't begin to tell you how nice it's been to have other people in our group, especially a woman."

Menace clutched Solace tighter. "There are other females on my planet."

"Each sinkhole that opens and we slip through has gone from hope to horror for me now that I finally have my boy back," Joe said. "Since his mother died, I've been so lost. That night Joey disappeared suddenly half my house was gone. Do you know what it's like to stare into a vortex, a black nothing and want to dive in headfirst? I'd just bathed him and tucked him in. He wanted one last story, but after five I said no. Do you know how often I wished I'd told him one last story?"

"Daddy?"

"Hmm?"

"Daddy my other people, the ones who said they were my parents didn't know any stories. At night I made up my own, the same one every night, and it came true, you came for me."

Joe hugged his son. Menace helped Solace settle the other children in the safety of the plane as the sun began to set. He then took her in his arms and cradled her against his chest.

"I feel like I'm in a story," Menace said. "An alien is manipulating our lives for its entertainment. What will happen next?"

"I guess everyone lives a story. The moment you're born a book opens. Each person begins a new chapter of their lives like in a book. Fate and destiny play their hand like an author spinning a tale."

"Clarity has a book. I saw it in her purse," Menace said.

"Consider yourself lucky she let you get that close to her purse. There are tazers in there. I almost zapped myself with her lipstick container. Doom rescued me. I'm guessing he got up close and personal with it once," Solace said.

Menace chuckled. "He sure did."

Solace rolled closer into his arms and she relaxed. Menace closed his eyes and hoped sleep wouldn't be elusive. Thoughts and ideas nagged at him. Clarity's book with the strange markings on them came to mind; she called them written words. *How do you write a word you speak into the air?* Menace felt a storybook would be better said with pictures. Either way, his thoughts were depressing.

"If you are writing my story, alien, fate, or destiny, make certain it has a happy ending," Menace whispered aloud. His eyes strained into the darkness. There wasn't a strange symbol to be seen. Clarity said words could be written in many languages. His head began to ache with his thoughts. Was a dog still a dog if the word was spoken differently? The people of the trees spoke in a number of strange languages from what Solace said. Perhaps it wasn't the words; it was understanding what was said.

"Alien if you are listening, I hope you can write my story in my language. If not maybe that's why strange things happen that I don't understand." The idea filled his thoughts for a long time and sleep was as elusive as he speculated it to be.

****

When morning came his arm was numb, Menace

hadn't wanted to disturb Solace's sleep. He watched as the sun rose to dazzle the highlights in her hair. Lips begged to be kissed in the slight pout she wore, and he wondered what she was dreaming of. Today he would find a quiet pool to bathe in, a secluded place where he would wash her flesh until she tingled with deep desire. His fingers would dance over her skin making her whimper with want. Menace wanted to watch her sweet nipples harden until…

"Do you think Bongo, Muffin and Bubble-gum are all right?" Em interrupted Menace's train of thought.

Solace groaned, then squirmed. "Am I sitting on the gun?"

"No," Menace said, teeth pressed tight together, she was killing him. Then, "I'm certain Doom has been watching over everyone, Em."

The others began to stir and Joe handed out dried mammoth meat. But Solace refused and with a smile reminded them breakfast was in the ground. Later for lunch was soon enough for dried meat.

"We could make a stew from the meat if we find fresh water, and Solace is adept at finding greens and other edible vegetation." Menace shifted Solace into a more comfortable position; food was the last thing on his mind. He was concentrating on taking her away. Solace rose to her feet and sent him a saucy gaze. She knew what he had in mind. There was no missing the bulge in his pants.

Menace followed her outside. The day dawned bright and clear which made Joe grumble it was an awesome day for flying. Solace and Menace dug the food out from the ground. The idea worked and the emu was delicious. There were many roots and a few greens as well. They ended their meal with nuts. Menace was antsy to be away and reminded Solace about the water. He remembered flying over a pond. They gathered the flasks and water skins they had.

"Yeah and we should all wash up. It might get a little smelly in here with us all," Bastian said. "I miss those hot springs in the treehouse. Normally a woman would find me eventually. Which wasn't too horrible."

"I'm certain your sacrifice will be remembered fondly," Tain said dryly.

"Just takin' one for the team," Bastian replied with a quick smile.

"One?" Lochlan said and raised a brow.

"I think Solace and I will look for water today, alone," Menace said, their references weren't subtle to him, though over the heads of the children. He was remembering a few times with him and Solace in a few of their spring fed waters.

"I think the kids and I should gather firewood and make a signal fire in case there are others and to keep predators away," Joe said. "Yesterday was a long walk."

"Tain and I can go look in a different direction today. Lochlan why don't you stay and help Joe? That way we're all armed," Bastian said.

"Sounds like a plan," Lochlan said. He glanced at Menace mischievously and said, "Don't make us have to come look for you."

Menace smiled. "I can kill a raptor barehanded."

Solace grinned at the exchange. As she and Menace headed out she punched Lochlan in the arm.

"It's true. He can reach right inside and rip the heart from an exposed cavity."

"Good to know," Lochlan said as he watched them leave.

Menace took Solace by the hand. The area they traveled was clear with a few trees and shrubbery. He was wishing they were home. The hot springs would have been welcome. There was a gentle breeze that fluttered Solace's hair. Menace chose to go bare-chested. Solace was using a leather bag to carry edible vegetation she found including nuts and berries placed in different compartments.

"If the aliens can open a sinkhole do you think they brought us here?" Solace said.

"Maybe," Menace replied. He frowned. "I hope they aren't watching us somehow."

"Thanks for creeping me out. I need to pee."

"I thought your humans were watched all year long? When sleeping and awake."

"What makes you think that?" She chuckled. "Drones, spies, Big Brother?"

"Santa Claus."

Solace howled with laughter much to his surprise. She dropped her carrying bag and slipped behind a tree. Menace waited patiently. Watched or not when you gotta go, you gotta go. She emerged still smiling and tightened the leather draw cord at the waist of her hide pants. She tromped beside him in her leather shoes given to her from the treehouse people. She was in a hide shirt made of megaceros de-haired.

"The aliens have been sufficiently mooned," she declared. "Remind me on our way back to grab more of the leaves out here. They're super soft. God, how I miss toilet paper."

"What are those?"

Solace and he stopped to watch a herd of a massive beast. "Wow those are big. Big even for bison. Supersized. They are typically wild and wouldn't rely on humans on my earth. But those are badass." She gazed at him and she must have seen his curiosity. "This must be as much of a culture shock to you as your planet was to me."

"You seem comfortable here looking at beasts I've never set eyes on before."

She went on to explain the bison were almost twice as large as their predecessors and hugely shaggy. The small herd of perhaps twenty grazed on the lush grass.

"There must be water to support such beasts." Menace took her hand and they continued to look. Past the herd and over a small hill they found a secluded pond with a marsh beyond. Long high stems rose and waved in a slight breeze. Massive trees with long hanging branches swished the water with their tips. Cattails were near the water's edge and Menace wanted to take a bunch back to the plane, this was a plant he knew was edible and he knew how to roast the stalks.

Menace stripped but Solace hung back looking worried. "Menace you don't know what's in there."

"Water is in there."

"What if turtles are in there? Snappers the likes we've never seen, or leeches the size of snakes."

Menace smiled and held out his hand. He was waist deep. "My planet has dinosaurs."

"Sometimes your fearlessness is scary."

She let go of her leather bag and stripped her hide pants off first, the rest of the garments followed. Naked she shivered as she went to him. She buried her face into his chest and he wrapped his arms around her.

126

Tenderly he cupped her chin to have her meet his gaze.

"I will not lose you to a turtle or any other beast. I will not lose you to an alien, or dinosaur or hybrid. What I will do is live inside you. As long as you carry me in your heart I am alive. There is no one on any planet more important to me than you. You are my everything and the most beautiful woman I have ever set eyes on."

Solace smiled. "You're right. I don't think there's a kickass dinosaur alive that can evict you."

"No matter where we are we are one. If you could feel the love I carry for you you'd need to be a brontosaurus to carry it all."

"I think our love lifts me higher and makes my steps lighter. Love is an emotion of strength not weight."

Menace grinned. "Then you have the power of a full grown mammoth mastodon with you."

"A mammadon."

"Not a mastomoth?"

She chuckled making her features light with delight. He was thrilled she loved him. Menace bent to taste her sweet lips. He reached down to cup water to pour over her flesh and she shivered. The droplets glided over her breasts and dripped from a puckered nipple. He bent his head to lap at her. When he released her, they took turns washing each other with water and their hands. He wanted to feel every inch of her and he did before slipping a finger deep into her warm wet heat. Her hands clutched his shoulders as she moved with him. Menace picked her up and settled them at the base of a willow tree.

The grass was soft under his back as he sat Solace

over him. She helped guide him where they both needed him to be. She gasped as he plunged hard pulling her down. He reached to knead her breasts in each hand. Solace tossed her head back moaning, rocking in a loving rhythm. It was his turn to groan when her insides squeezed and released. Menace rolled them over and she wrapped her legs around his waist.

Every inch of him buried to the hilt until he withdrew his throbbing cock. He plunged again loving she could take all of him. Menace gripped her silky hair to tilt her neck back. He nipped her throat to her jaw. He was ready and wanted to make certain she was. She quivered with need and Menace thrust harder.

"I love you, Solace." Her body shook and he felt his juices spurt. Their climax was quiet but no less powerful.

She smiled at him and traced his cheek with her finger. "I love you my powerful warrior. I will follow you from the ends of one planet to the ends of another, as long as it takes, wherever it takes us."

Menace grinned at her then released her. He dragged her to her feet and told her to hurry. After she claimed the aliens might be guiding them, he realized she was not only right, but also why they were brought here. Out of fuel rendering the plane useless.

"What is it?" she asked.

"One planet to another no matter what it takes," he said. "You reminded me of something. A hybrid came through the sinkhole with me but we separated. The aliens are guiding us. They brought us here and I think I know why. The hybrid is here, Solace. This is where the fight will begin and end."

Menace took up her leather satchel and the pair

sprinted off together.

****

"Are you certain there's a hybrid here?" Joe asked.

"If Menace says there's one you better believe him. Those beasts are dangerous and they can think," Solace said. "The males are at least eight feet tall, built like tanks, show zero mercy, and will eat your brains from your head while you're still alive if given the chance."

"Well then we won't give the bastard a chance. We'll blow it away," Lochlan said.

"I'll kill the fucker all right," Menace said. He swung his sword.

"What if it's seen us using the weapons, the guns?" Solace said.

"I'm guessing it has," Menace said. "It knows we are dangerous. It will find out how to be more dangerous. It has seen me battle with my weapon."

"We better find a way out of here then," Tain said.

"No," Menace said. "If the aliens brought us here we won't be going anywhere until we kill it. The hybrid cannot have the plane. It must die. I need to learn a new way to hunt to surprise it."

"Then I say we all hunt it," Lochlan said.

Solace was worried. She was female and she knew the hybrid was too big to breed with her but would still kill the men and eat their brains. If it could figure a way to impregnate her and wait a few years the children would grow up to provide new sacrifices. Could the hybrid be smart enough to cultivate humans?

It already has.

She shuddered with the thought. The beast would keep the children alive then use them when they aged, breeding them and once children were born he would kill off the parents until all humans ever knew would be of a hybrid ruler. The hybrid would study the plane until it could figure out flight. Joey might even be able to help him if his father was gone and there were no adults to turn to for protection.

The men were planning a hunt. Menace wanted to be taught how to use a machine gun. He had a sword and small weapons, his knife and the one special tool made for him for skinning a hide. The hybrid would rip him to shreds if he had to fight bare handed but Menace said the beast watched him use his sword. What was needed was surprise.

"We can give you a crash course, Menace," Lochlan said.

Menace shuddered. "I don't want to learn to crash. The plane goes way too high." Lochlan and Bastian chuckled.

"A fast course in guns," Lochlan said.

"What if," Solace began, interrupting them while they spoke of guns. "What if we were never going to be allowed to take the plane back to Menace's planet. Nothing goes through on his planet except humans. Doom said he was surprised Clarity came through with her purse. Same with the earth dog, Bubble-gum is unique."

"Clarity wasn't meant to go to our planet. She said the aliens made a mistake and battled to return her somewhere else," Menace said. "You know Clarity. She won't take shit from anything."

"That's why she disappeared," Nina said as though enlightened. "I got jolted in a bomb blast and she and I hid in a tree. A hole opened and she was gone but she came back before I could tell anyone."

"How did she disappear?" Solace asked.

"The ground swallowed her but she shoved me back. Then the earth stopped rumbling and levelled off. I couldn't dig her up." Nina had tears streaming down her face. "I ran to get help but everyone was fighting. There was so much blood, and then Clarity was back and the plane came shooting out of the ground. I didn't want to leave Kiki and Luke behind but I wanted to go home so bad. Nick and the twins and Joey were on the plane, and you Solace. I at least had half my family."

"Not Nina fault," Nick said.

Solace startled at the compassion in his voice. The teen had made the children his family. He took care of them; he loved them. Nick held Nina for a moment. He was awkward with his bent arms, but everyone was moved. A scary thought occurred to Solace. If Clarity could be grabbed so easily, what was to stop the aliens from taking the rest of them and leaving Menace to fight alone? He couldn't without a gun. The Neandersauri knew Menace's skill with a sword; she wouldn't take the chance of him being so close to the hybrid. She turned to Lochlan.

"You need to teach Menace to shoot. *Now*."

Menace placed his hand on her shoulder. "I can see what you're thinking. We can only hope we all end up together."

"What, what is she thinking?" Bastian asked.

"That the sinkholes will begin opening here," Menace said.

"If the children start to disappear we won't know if it's the hybrid or the aliens. My God what a crazy world we've all been tossed into," Solace said.

"Will the aliens send us home?" Em asked. "Mine

was a mess. Going to Doom would be better."

"Daddy don't let them take me away again," Joey howled.

"You need to stay with us," Blue cried out and both he and Cole wrapped little arms around Menace's legs.

The entire plane was in an uproar. Until Menace made a loud whistle. He gazed at everyone.

"If any of you suddenly find yourself on a strange planet filled with dinosaurs find Doom. He will take care of you."

"What if we're sent all over? I'll be all alone," Em said.

Menace disengaged the boys and dropped to a knee before her. "We will find you. Solace and I found each other. I will vow to not stop looking for you. For any of you children."

The other children crowded around him when he picked up Em and sat her on his knee. Even Nick hovered looking worried. Tain grabbed a machine gun.

"Let's get busy. We need to teach the big guy how to use this puppy."

Everyone filed outside and stayed close.

"Do you think anything will happen today?" Nina said.

Menace and Tain were quickly surrounded by the other men who were soon giving Menace pointers on how to use the machine gun. Solace could have helped but knew the children were on edge. The young teen was wringing her hands. Solace placed her hands on her shoulders.

"You are a brave young lady, Nina. All of you children are brave. Look at what you've been through. You have battled in a war, you've made weapons on

Doom's planet and you are all loyal. I think if the alien is manipulating things he will begin taking us when the hybrid is close or gearing up for an attack."

"Will he send us to Doom?" A little voice piped up. Solace crouched and picked up Blue.

"I don't know, sweetheart. Menace and I will find you no matter what happens."

"Me too?" Cole held his arms up to her.

Solace smiled and hefted him to her hip. "We're a team you guys. Before when the sinkholes took you from our Earth it was scary because you didn't know what was going on. We're ready this time. We have each other."

Solace took in their wary faces. She kissed Cole's forehead then Blue's. She wondered if knowing *was* for the best. Time would tell. The first to disappear was Em. Nina screamed as a dark hole hovered over the child's head while sitting on a tree branch watching Menace learn to shoot. Nina reached for her, they clasped hands as Menace raced to them, shouting at them to go to Doom, they must go to Doom. Solace wasn't certain if it was the aliens he was calling to or the children.

Joe strode to his son and picked him up. Solace doubted the boy's feet would ever hit the ground again. She didn't blame Joe for a second knowing he would travel to every planets hell if he had to if he must find his son again.

"So that's it?" Tain raged. "They pick us off one by one? This fucking sucks."

The sinkhole that took the girls was gone and a clear blue sky was overhead. Everyone was stunned. Nick had a hand to his mouth and Solace was certain he held back sobs. The pain etched on his face made him appear to be the helpless teen he was.

"I lost them," the teen muttered. "Lost many."

"This is beyond your control," Solace said to comfort him. "There are times life is not in your control."

"You mean Doom," his tone was that of rage. "I not Doom." Nick stormed off.

"You may need more than a gun, to kill the hybrid," Lochlan said as they watched Nick stomp his way into the plane pulling the twins with him.

"Like what?" Menace asked.

"Like a bomb," Joe said.

"We don't have bombs here and less time to make them," Solace said.

Joe gazed at the plane. He sighed as he ran a hand over the sleek metal. "This pile of junk and I have been friends for a long time. We have rope. We need some fat or something that burns steady."

Solace caught his idea. If all else failed Menace would need to blow up the plane. They set to work on a long rope coated in mammoth fat and tree pitch. Menace would need to get as far away as possible once the rope was lit. They worked closely together. The hybrid could be watching Menace learn to shoot and would understand the weapon was dangerous but it had never seen a plane and wouldn't know it could blow.

"Hey, guys." Solace gazed at Joe, Bastian, Lochlan and Tain. "I want to say I'm happy I met you. Not the circumstances, but pleased to know you nonetheless. My father was army; he would have been honored to have you on his team."

"I've got your back," Lochlan said then grinned.

"Until it vanishes anyway."

"I hope you and Menace get to where you need to be," Joe said, he carried his son in his arms, Solace was surprised he could hold the boy for so long. It was apparent Joe was never going to lose his boy again.

"We will," Menace said. "Please know you are all welcome on my planet. If there is where you end up, I would be pleased to have you in my village, and so would Doom."

"We best get some rest," Tain said. Solace smiled at him. He was a quiet complex man, never making mention of loved ones or home.

"If we are being taken where do you want to end up, Tain?" she asked.

"Anywhere I can shoot my gun."

"What about you, Joe?" Solace asked.

"A quiet place to raise my son." He smiled slightly then followed Tain into the plane.

"Well Bastian, you're next," Lochlan said. "Where do you want your hide going?"

"Joe and I have been friends a long time. Wherever he goes is fine, as long as there are lots of women."

Lochlan chuckled. "I have no ties on my earth," Lochlan said. "I'd kinda like to meet the dude called Doom." He winked at Solace and they went to the plane followed by Menace.

The twin boys disappeared overnight with Nick. Solace's insides were in an uproar. She was reminded of a story by Agatha Christie—*And Then There Were None*. All were on edge. She was loath to release Menace's hand for a second but he was learning about a weapon he obviously fell in love with. Tain was giving more instructions to Menace when a vortex opened and he was sucked in, howling, leaving the gun behind. Solace was in a panic. Menace was catching on fast but she was terrified she would be next to go. Joe and his son disappeared together during the next night, followed quickly by Lochlan.

"Why is it the black dude is always the last to go?" Bastian complained. "Aliens can't handle me, that's why. Too smart for them, too handsome, too…"

He was still complaining when he stepped from the plane and the ground swallowed him. Solace stood looking at Menace.

"We need to take a stand. The hybrid must be close. If we can spot him before he spots us, it would be better." He nodded.

Menace raced them to the pond where at the marsh they turned over rocks to step in the depression, then settled the rocks back into position to hide their tracks. Menace turned to Solace. He crushed her into his embrace. His thumbs stroked her cheeks.

"You know that no matter what I will always find you." She nodded. "I live in you. Keep me safe. That means you must be safe at all cost, my love. I couldn't bear to be without you. You are everything to me. You are warmth and beauty, passion, and power. I am honored with your love. I have never been happier than when I am with you. Do you know I never smiled as a child or an adult until I met you? The first time was so foreign to me I was afraid, yes afraid. It was as though I walked from darkness into light, I could see, Solace. My heart opened, you did that. Can you even guess how special you make my world and those around you? Be safe, my love."

He pressed his forehead to hers and rubbed her

cheek with a thumb. She smiled while trying not to cry. This time they were prepared to be parted; it didn't sting less. Solace sucked in her breath gazing beyond him. The hybrid was coming, racing along the marsh; it must have been watching them. Huge legs took long strides. Menace turned to look when she pointed. When he glanced to where Solace once stood, she was gone.

Chapter Nine

Solace gazed at her surroundings. She wasn't on any planet. There didn't appear to be a floor beneath her feet but she was on solid ebony ground. Her reflection gazed up at her as she studied where she stood. She was standing in a massive room watching earths, twenty of them—no nineteen, as one disintegrated into particles—hover and circle her, from everywhere. Each planet appeared close enough to touch, such was the illusion. She was in semi-darkness. The planets, all different colors, with some being larger, spun lazily. Each planet was in possession of at least one sun, and moon. Solace turned at the deep voice of a male. A cloak covered him from head to toe.

"Don't be afraid."

"Which is the planet Menace is on right now?"

He pointed to a larger planet. "The same type of fiery meteors that hit your Earth in the early thousand year beginnings hit their Earth but with the different DNA building blocks to create life. It was too flawed. There was too much illness, sadness, more so than your Earth. The humanoids warred often and died young. People gave up on hope. Some sat in corners wishing for death, others crumpled where they stood watching gangs who committed cruelties. The DNA mix was no good. Exaggerated evil mixed with meek. I couldn't take the suffering.

"It was time to call them back to us. There is no one left on that planet and we have yet to decide what to do with it and some of the people who wait in limbo for our decision. The planet will postpone life for a few hundred thousand years. We may add other species first. Before we introduce any signs of human life we will wait until all traces of the others vanish. Your Earth taught us that. Pyramids, Stonehenge, and other phenomenon. Humans are so inquisitive. At times they can be delightful, others exasperating."

"Which am I?"

"Both."

"Menace is alone on that planet with a hybrid from his world."

"The hybrid he fell into the sinkhole with was sent onto another planet, that one, for safe keeping. The Neandersauri must be dispatched. It is unfortunate but the creature cannot stay there. I didn't know where else to send it. I am hopeful Menace will be victorious but you humans have taken much of my time. I have others to settle."

"Then why did you take me from Menace?"

"You are not meant to die on that planet."

"Is Menace?"

"Menace is supposed to go home. He carries too many lives on his person to simply lose. I need a home for those souls as well."

Something about his tone bothered her. "Did you return the others to Doom's planet?"

"Some. Tain and Bastian are headed to a new destiny. The father of the one we want for our new planet will stay with his child. We came to the conclusion there could be no separating of the two. Joe would go after his son again and Doom's planet is no place for either. The new planet they were sent is not in infancy, but rather in a far more advanced state, something the boy needs. Do not fear for them, they will be fine. I anticipate Joe's reaction to flight and the manner in which it's done on his new world."

"What about Doom's planet?"

"The hybrids are too dangerous, but Doom is winning the war. Unfortunately it won't be of consequence. Something not foreseen but not at all unusual either will happen. There is a planet on a collision course with his planet."

"What?" she shrieked. "Make it stop."

"The two colliding planets will merge and create different life."

"Yes and will kill everyone on the planet. Are you so callous about life?"

"I adore life. If there was a way to stop the planet we would. The collision is not of our doing."

"The sinkholes…"

"The sinkholes are unfortunate and somewhat unstable. I am also not the cause of all of them. Other aliens play a factor. I can't suddenly open a bunch of holes and drop Doom's people in. I already have a wayward hybrid; I can't risk more falling through. The sinkhole wasn't meant to take the Neandersauri and I can't direct a sinkhole to a dead or dying planet. Menace and you could have been happy on the planet of All Humans, where you were welcomed, but it wasn't to be. Menace's drive is too strong; his loyalty to his planet and Doom runs deep. We are also not without the fond hand of fate interfering at times, annoying as it is."

He waved his arm in a different direction to send Solace to gaze at a higher planet. One more earth was on the verge of death, it was turning gray.

"What about the people on that planet?" she asked.

"The humans and inhabitants are long gone. Fate had a hand in that."

"So once all of your Earths die the human race will be gone?" Solace asked.

"No, planets form all the time, they grow and expand. See the dead Earth is gone, deteriorated and is now dust and particles. Everything is floating. All of the debris will reassemble with crucial DNA to form another Earth and Earth-like planets. The planets will have their own species. Even the dead and buried take something of themselves to new worlds. You are never really gone. Dinosaur bones, fossils should have taught you that."

"Roaming planets?"

"Orphan worlds, planemo, planets with no stars will sling shot each other."

"Sling shot?" Solace's thoughts began to race.

"Those worlds can move into our system and we can nurture life, give the planets a home. They are without an owner and yet to be molded."

Solace went to stare at Menace's world. She could see a meteor would be directly beside the planet before being struck by the wayward planet. The meteor would align with the wayward planet for a brief moment.

"You can manipulate the new planet. You can sling shot the meteor against the other planet like in the game of pool and move Doom's planet those few inches out of reach. You can change the gravitational pull for a few seconds. That's all we need, a tiny tap from the meteor not a collision with the huge planet. The meteor can be a go between. We just got our proverbial fulcrum and lever."

"I beg your pardon?"

"Archimedes said, 'Give me a fulcrum and a lever and I can move the world.' Let's move the world— Doom and Menace's world, a few inches."

"Moving an established earth with a moon and sun and gravitational pull could have devastating effects."

"Oh, and having a planet crash and kill everyone won't."

"The timing is everything. The meteor would have to rap the planet a millisecond before the collision. The gravitational sling shot would then have to pull Doom's earth back into place again a millisecond after the meteor and planet pass."

"But you can do it?'

"Yes but…"

"Do it, damn you. Set it up."

"I've seen your pool games dearie, and remember the black ball."

"Then think of it as a pretty pink planet."

"The shift will pull Doom's earth toward the moon and it will be high tide when the change occurs. You could be looking at substantial flooding."

"Yes but the flooding will recede?"

"Technically yes. A hypercane could form, volcanoes will erupt when none had. Continents will split. There could be an ice age."

"Then send me there to warn the villagers to get to higher ground and get provisions ready."

"That isn't possible."

"Why not?"

"I explained to Clarity she wasn't supposed to be there."

"She came back."

"She is on a collision course with a planet."

"What is so different about her and me?"

"Your blood type. The RH negative factor was never to mix with this planet. We tried it on your Earth thousands of years ago, then again on another planet. On your planet there is a color war, a religious war. Fighting is also on the other planet. Just think of being separated from your mother at birth because you are O positive or O negative. A virtual blood war where no one cares about the color of your skin or religion any more than they would care if grass is green. We decided not to do it again."

"How do you know I'm not supposed to be on Doom's planet? What if there is a higher power that directs even you?"

"Interesting concept. Perhaps true."

"Send me back."

"You could die."

"I want to be with Menace. I need to warn the others."

"It's admirable you are willing to risk your life. Are you willing to risk the life of your baby?"

That stopped her in her tracks. "My, *my* baby?"

"You carry life, Solace. I can detect a force within you. Small as yet but there is something there. You have some time to decide. Come, eat. Rest. Your warrior needs to concentrate on the hybrid. I will send him a sign you are well. In the meantime I see a game of pool in my future."

****

Menace panicked. He knew Solace would be taken from him, but to where? The hybrid was gaining ground. The wind picked up. The tingling of icy fear invaded his heart for her. What if she were tossed into a battle unarmed? How could he function without his love, how could he not? It was up to him alone to defeat the Neandersauri. He couldn't let all earths down he needed to focus.

"I will not fail Solace. I will not."

A small flower fluttered to the ground near his feet. Solace's favorite kind. Menace looked up in time to see the remains of a dark hole close. The flower was from his world. Did it mean Solace was safely back on his planet with Doom, waiting for him? Menace hoped so. The gift was enough to focus on what needed to be done. The sooner he killed the beast the sooner he would learn Solace's fate.

The machine gun in his hand set off popping noises as he aimed for the hybrid who was fast approaching. The beast raised a shield last moment, it looked to be a rusted car door, and what Menace had thought to be an easy kill wasn't so easy. The beast kept coming, his long legs eating up the terrain. The shield lowered slightly and there was an evil grin on the beast's face. Menace should have known the being was clever. Menace turned and it was his turn to let his feet fly over the land. He had to get behind the beast or over it.

Heart hammering in his chest, he had never pumped his legs so brutally fast. The plane came into view. The engine was destroyed, completely gutted with the parts cooked black in the ground oven Solace made days earlier. They would take no chances. A group of five massive dogs attacked and Menace wielded the gun taking the lives of two. The beasts howled and backed off to go after the hybrid. Menace jumped into the plane, his sword swinging at his side from his belt, he needed both hands to hold the gun. He watched as the hybrid smashed the dogs with the car door, into the face, onto a head, making them cry out in pain, and a thought occurred to Menace.

As the hybrid lifted the door to send another dog flying, Menace fired on his enemy. He'd thought to take the beast out with a clean shot. He was a skilled hunter and the idea filling him was enlightening. Menace wasn't in need of a compassionate execution. The beast was his enemy, not mere prey or food. The bullets hit along the hybrid's left side from ankle to hip. The hybrid went down as bone shattered. The Neandersauri bellowed in fury and agony. The beast crushed the third dog by crashing the door onto its back. Exposed for mere seconds, Menace rattled off another burst. The hybrid jerked as he was hit in his hip and right arm. Menace slammed the plane door closed as the hybrid rose to his feet and began to run for him.

As the beast smashed repeatedly into the door rocking the plane, Menace tried to slip from the broken window at the front of the plane. His belt caught, and he was stuck. He pushed the machine gun out ahead of him and taking his dagger, he sliced his belt off. The sword rattled when it hit the ground and Menace broke free, he swore. He couldn't go in after it. The hybrid battled the door mercilessly, shaking the plane. Menace stood above the hybrid, his feet braced, he took aim and fired. Nothing happened. He tried again, nothing. The gun wasn't empty; Tain mentioned something about a gun being jammed. Menace didn't know how to fix it.

He swore under his breath and shook the gun. Nothing.

The plane was quaking with the determination of the hybrid who took no notice of the man above him, tossing Menace back and forth on the balls of his feet until he crouched. Murderous talon claws squealed over the metal making flying sparks, the noise was deafening. The claws hooked into the door and the mind numbing sound as the door was peeled back grated on Menaces nerves. The hybrid succeeded in opening the door, tossing it aside with such force the metal flew over the tops of trees.

Once inside, Menace could feel the beast searching for him. Overhead hatches inside the plane were ripped off their hinges and thrown at the smaller windows. Menace was stretched out, peeking inside upside down from the shattered window. Seats went flying out the gaping door hole. The beast roared from the back of the plane. With only seconds left before detection, Menace rose and skidded down the side of the plane and raced to a woven vine coated in pitch and mammoth fat. Using the lighter Lochlan gave him, Menace set it on fire—and ran. The rope-vine wasn't long and he could hear it hissing its way along the ground. The other end of the rope was attached to the fuel tank. They had run on fumes but Joe informed him there was just enough to make an explosion, and to make sure he was nowhere near the plane when it went off.

Menace heard the pounding of his heart as his feet connected with the ground. His fists were balled as he raced, head forward. The blast, when it came, blew him to the ground where he somersaulted, was airborne, then hit the earth with a groan. Black smoke billowed to rise high disrupting the clear sky. His ears were ringing.

Pieces of plane were tossed high into the air. The head of the hybrid landed beside him giving him a jolt. The tail of the plane was headed right for Menace. There was no way he could escape. He bellowed Solace's name and felt the ground give way beneath him. The tail bounced on the place Menace once sat, the sinkhole already closed over his head.

Menace was sailing through the air, coughing dust from his mouth and nose. Guts in a knot he was standing as his feet slipped along a dark hole. The light ahead was blinding as he shot forward bellowing. His target was unfortunate but unavoidable. A surprised Doom caught him as they crashed to the ground. Doom tossed him off and rose grabbing a sword.

"Well shit, Menace, say your hello with words next time. You weigh more than a mammoth mastodon."

Menace jumped up and found a sword. He sliced through a hybrid behind Doom and gave him a cocky grin.

"I missed you."

Doom rolled his eyes. "See how easy that was." He clapped him on the back and returned to the battle.

****

"Have you made your decision?" the alien asked Solace.

"Yes. I choose to go to Doom's planet."

"There will be devastation."

"I'm certain of it. All of this," she waved a hand, "shows me I am meant to do something, to be somewhere. I need to be with Menace."

"Daddy's little warrior."

Solace raised her chin. "Yes I am."

"So be it."

"Wait," she said. "Please, I must know. The children I was with when I first fell into a sinkhole. What happened to them? Was it your sinkhole or did another alien race grab them?"

The alien appeared to ponder her question. "It was mine. Had you stayed longer, you would have seen them on the ancient planet you encountered. The planet you were destined for until something went wrong as it did with Clarity."

"But we were with humans, and the children are not Neanderthals. I didn't see any of them."

"There was mention of another human in that era. Humans that will decide to move away. Children, with the knowledge of another place deep-seated in their young minds will save the people they were given to because they have a memory of the safety of walls, homes. The idea of markets will emerge. The concept of villages will spread."

"There were only a few who were taken. Can a few do so much?"

The alien laughed. "You have, Clarity has. The little ones are loved, they've already adapted to their new life. The choice to take them was made when their parents died." Solace gaped. "You seem surprised. They, their parents, were all killed the same day, a mass shooting spree. You were important to the children on Earth. You helped them to become what they must while in your care for so short a time. You did well. Now you have done well for other children."

"Why was I supposed to go to that Earth with the daycare children?"

"You would have remained with Dagger. Did you not see his interest in you? If there was no Menace, well. Dagger's people will never leave. Any offspring you would have had would have remained."

Solace swallowed hard, Dagger was open with information and kind. If Menace wasn't there, if she had never met him—but she *had* met Menace. "The people would have gone unnoticed. My offspring and theirs would never have been found if I remained with Dagger. There isn't any record of that type of people on my Earth."

"Exactly. Perhaps you are right about the hand of fate of another being interfering in what was originally planned for you. It is why we will risk your DNA to be introduced. You have tremendous spirit and will. Your bravery supersedes many. You will need it."

Solace was humbled. Yes, during history at times it took only one voice to be heard, as long as it was loud enough and kept on making sound. She smiled, recalling some of the words to a song from her Earth, 'I might only have one match, but I can make an explosion.'

The alien bade her to step into a chamber. Solace lost her stomach into a knot as she was dropped, plunged straight down. Fast curves followed, loop de loops. The speed slowed and she braced herself, holding her hands protectively across her belly. When she landed, she bounced off a furry bulwark who groaned, raised a massive claw, snorted in surprise, and then licked her instead.

"Love me later, Muffin," she said, shoving the beast aside. She was in the middle of a war zone. Humans and hybrids battled.

She saw Kiki and Luke in their favorite back-to-back stance. Bongo the massive cave hyena was close as was Rex the tiny T-rex. Doom caught her eye and he gazed at her for a second in surprise. Solace raced forward and grabbed a sword from the ground. She engaged with a young hybrid.

"My destiny is to live," the hybrid howled with fewer whistles and more words which startled her for a mere second.

"Your destiny is to die," Solace bellowed.

"Bite me."

"I don't lick assholes. I sure as hell ain't gonna bite one."

The hybrid howled in rage at the taunt. His fury clouded his mind, and Solace sliced through his open arms as they raised, poised to strike. She watched him drop to his knees. A bellow behind her and Solace spun. Menace was there slicing off the clawed hand of a hybrid before it could strike her. Her first instinct was to race into his arms but this wasn't the time. She filled with pride knowing he had beaten the hybrid on the lonely planet.

She gazed around but didn't see Nina or Em; she hoped they were in hiding. Lochlan was in battle. No sign of Joey or Joe. She remembered the alien saying there would be no chance of the aliens getting vital flight information. Tain and Bastian were absent. She would miss them and hoped they were well. Lochlan swung the sword he held as though born to it. The man did love a good fight. She wasn't certain but she thought she saw Nick weave in and out of the trees. The teen was a shadow in this world; he knew every nook and cranny. Solace was happy for him. Time would tell if his fiery hatred of Doom had cooled.

As if by collective agreement a large whistle blew

and the hybrids retreated to lick their wounds. There were fallen humans with hybrids. The leaders of other villagers gathered their dead and retreated. The bodies would be burned. The humans didn't want dinosaurs to discover a fondness for human flesh.

Solace was engulfed by Menace's arms. "I was so worried," he said, his chest heaving. He crushed her to him and she held him as tight.

"There is so little time and so much to say." Solace called to Doom.

Doom hugged her, as did the others. "It's time to eat and rest," Doom shouted.

"It's time to head to higher ground." Solace's tone was urgent. "We need to get home now because I have something I need to tell all of you, fast."

Solace took Menace by the hand and urged everyone to get to shelter, she had a message all villages needed to hear. Gathered together in the main hall Solace gazed at familiar faces and a few not as familiar. Leaders of other closer villages joined them. She stood on the table to gain everyone's attention.

"We have a more serious problem than the Neandersauri," she called out scanning the people. All of Doom's men were over six foot four, with Doom the largest at six foot six. All men were bald. Menace was the one with the most intricate tattoos. Solace would have been startled by Doom's lack of tattoos if Menace hadn't previously explained about the aliens. The village women were all close to six feet with long flowing white hair. Other Earth humans were small in number.

"Before coming here I was privy to an alien's prediction. A planet is on a collision course with this one. The alien has agreed to try and manipulate a meteor to hit this planet, bounce this world by tapping it out of the planets way then dragging it back to space on the tail of the other planets gravitational pull. There will be devastating side effects. You will experience nature at its worst. Tidal waves, tsunamis, volcanoes once dormant will rise. Tornadoes, hurricanes, weather changes of huge proportions. Flooding so severe it could cut everyone off from other villages."

"What would happen if the other planet hit us?" Doom asked.

"Total annihilation. This is the only way we can survive, or at least try to. We need to plan. We need to get everything together, food, shelter, water," Solace insisted.

"How do we fight the hybrids?" Edge yelled. "They live in the mountains."

"By telling them nothing," Clarity shouted. "We don't fight. Let them think we are on the run, or regrouping. We go into hiding, and we plan, and more importantly, we all move to higher ground. The higher the better. Much higher than the hybrids have ever gone. Way up into the mountain peaks if possible. The hybrids are wary of returning to their homes as it is because of our attacks."

Solace sighed with relief when her friend backed her up.

"Will our homes not be safe?" Doom asked. "Nothing can penetrate them."

"How long are you willing to be trapped if we're covered by an ocean for a hundred years?" Solace asked. "What will we do for food if trapped too long? How could we breathe? Could we? Think hard about your ventilation system. Being safe and snug is fine, but how do we tell when or if it's safe to come out without letting the water in or a tide of waiting hybrids? Continents will form. Islands could rise from the ocean, and pieces of land may split and sink. There will be a new definition to this planet when everything settles. I hope it settles."

Clarity jumped up beside her. "We need somewhere to watch the storms. The first few days will bring the most destruction. If these homes still stand we can return later. Right now we better batten down the hatches in a new home, a higher home."

The leaders of the other villages rushed off to warn their own people, runners would be sent farther afield. Food was brought out as people now sat at the tables discussing the highest point and the safest route.

"I know highest closest mountain." The voice was Nick. Solace saw him on the floor surrounded by the other children, the twins, Nina, Em, Kiki, and Luke plus others not of her Earth. Solace was happy to see the ones she loved made it back, though Aba was silent, and Edge was stone faced. Joey Jr. remained with his father on another planet. The boy was never meant to be theirs, but the loss on their faces was apparent, and she hurt for them.

"Will you take us there?" Doom asked Nick.

"I take."

"Nick," Solace said. "We need everyone to survive."

"I angry," Nick said. "I hurt. I see too much loss. Mine, yours, all. No loss."

Solace wasn't certain if the teen's need for revenge cooled or if he realized there was a bigger threat. Nick came back through the sinkhole with the boys. Cole sat sleeping on his lap. Kiki was almost touching the teen's shoulder with hers. Nick was part of their community, whether he liked it or not.

"We need to hunt continuously, and forage for what we need," Menace said.

"All of our food must be moved, and furs and cooking utensils," Doom added.

"Burnable fuel can be found, but what about water?" Solace asked, then guzzled a fair amount.

"Water inside mountain. Much snow higher," Nick said. "Cold, but ice can melt."

Getting word to other villages was necessary with their plans. The larger the number of humans surviving would give them an edge over the hybrids. The biggest problem was the most important. Too many humans with loaded provisions was bound to give them away.

"Why don't we be sneaky in the open?" Solace said.

"What do you mean?" Doom asked.

"We make the hybrids think we're planning to stand our ground in a certain area while the rest of us move everything. We'll need to look like we're trying to keep our actions secret. Along the trails to higher ground set the real traps. We can pick them off one by one." She looked at Nick. "Is there a way to take things into the mountain without being seen?"

Nick scoffed. "Nick not want be seen, he not seen."

"Then we welcome your help," Doom said.

"Not for you," Nick said and sneered. "For family."

"Whether or not you like it young man, you're family. You'll need to be when we're in confined

154

spaces," Menace said. "To keep all family secure we need to work as a team to keep all safe."

Solace heard the underlying threat. So apparently did Nick who scowled but nodded. They all went back to their meal while plotting deep into the night. Not only was there need for food, but Solace wanted to gather the massive Aloe Vera plants for medicinal purposes and many other leaves including mint. Her mind raced and took stock of what was needed.

Morning bustle had the village women with some human women and all the children except Luke and Kiki, bundled high with provisions. They followed Nick who carried nothing. The teen tired easily and it would be a long hike. The path he would lead the women to would take them higher without his aid. Once the women were high enough they would stay and organize inside the many caves Nick claimed existed. Nick was to return for the rest of them below.

Organized groups went to hunt with the bulwarks. Kiki and Luke set traps with a number of others with Bubble-gum and the cave hyena as lookout. They dug pit traps. The immobilizing blue rocks from the beach were carefully handled and set as traps. They didn't want to spend too much time on a bogus war zone but unobtrusively saw a few slinking hybrids watching. The villagers played dumb and appeared not to notice.

When Nick returned he carried the end of a long rope. He explained the rope was attached to many more, to form a pulley up the side of the mountain. The contraption was designed to haul weapons, food, and necessities up and down the mountain, hidden from plain view. There were cave intervals where the items were unloaded then reloaded onto another pulley.

Solace suggested egg sip wells, huge hollowed eggs filled with water and stoppered along the way to reduce the need to haul another burden. The wells could be placed along trails up the mountain and used when needed. Menace smiled and called her remarkable. Solace told him Sapiens meant wise, something he didn't know.

The hybrids were wary and regrouping. Solace knew they now traveled in groups of five but with diminishing numbers few sentries could afford to be waylaid. Tension was high as both sides wondered the best day to engage. Solace knew if she were watching she would hope the villagers were tired with their efforts.

In the sky the dark planet came ever closer over the few weeks that followed. The shift would occur soon. The other meteor wasn't visible but she knew it was out there. The alien would need to tap the meteor into the planet to send it off course and swing it into the wayward planet for the avoidance of a more serious collision. As Solace shielded her eyes Menace approached.

"We haven't much time. If the hybrids haven't noticed the approaching planet, they will now. I doubt we'll see the meteor. It's moving too fast, and compared to a planet it's small. It's time to tell Doom we need to go. We need a few days to get up the mountain," Solace said.

As they gathered for a last meal in their homes Doom advised everyone they weren't going to wait any longer. Under the darkness of night, with Nick in the lead, they traveled deep within the mountain carrying massive loads of meat and disassembling the pulleys as they went. Able to move quicker, each bulwark dragged a kill easily three times its size ahead of them. The first night was spent in a cavern halfway up the mountain. The next, a little higher. When they reached their destination, the hunters took the hides from the beasts, scarred after rough travel but useful. Partitions needed to be made, and the main openings sealed off for protection.

Solace slipped off into a small cavern for privacy. She took a torch and Bubble-gum. The dog sniffed her urine and whined. She patted his head.

"I'll tell him I'm pregnant later," she whispered, then smiled. "Well aren't you the little pregnancy test?"

She rejoined the group. Menace gave her a worried glance.

"Are you all right?" he asked. "That's three times in a short time."

"Nerves," she simply said. It was true. The world was about to go to shit and she had a baby on the way. Her nerves were shot.

"We'll be all right," Menace soothed, taking her into his arms and running his hands up and down her back.

Solace wasn't as sure. Menace had never seen the destruction of nature, only humans. Both were sad but unless a body was diseased a single death couldn't bring civilization to its knees. Mother Nature in all her glory could, and might.

Chapter Ten

They all felt it the second the meteor hit. For a moment, their surroundings were surreal as the planet moved, and the meteor tapped them. Then the gravity of the wayward planet pulled it back to settle where it once was. Birds flew in a panic, darkening the skies in a huge murmuration. Light in the distance was a brilliance of electrons. Her heart raced. Solace knew the meteor struck the other side of the planet, which was little consolation. All would suffer in some way. The effect was instantaneous. A sonic boom sounded, their ground quivered. Though far away, they saw the wave of the ocean water pull back farther and farther until it disappeared altogether leaving massive sea animals floundering. From their elevated position Lochlan let all take a look with binoculars.

"The water has been stolen," Edge said in disbelief. He pulled the binoculars from his face and stared at them in astonishment. Clarity took them from him.

"You will wish it had been in a moment," Clarity said. Solace heard the quiver in her tone. Doom wrapped his arm around Clarity.

"What is that?" Aba's loud whispered words trembled. A horrendous rushing sound could be heard.

"A water wall, it moves," Menace said.

Dinosaurs that were once milling in panic began racing, retreating at a sight they never before experienced. The massive tidal wave barreled across the lands, sweeping away everything in its path. Toppling mile high trees, mammoth mastodon hybrids struggled to stay afloat. The beasts trumpeted their terror, a sound pitiful and fueled with fright. A sob caught in Solace's throat, they tried to herd the regal beasts higher, but you do not tell a creature weighing tons where to go. They didn't dare start fires to herd them or the hybrids would know something was up. Everyone hoped a food source would not become extinct, everyone hoped humans would not become extinct.

From their view a few watched, others huddled together away from the sights of the planet's carnage. Brontosaurus floundered then went under, sucked high until smashed forward. Huge winged beasts squawked and flew into the darkening sky. On another high mountain was a race of giant mouflon hybrids struggling to safety in the snow-covered mountaintops. Solace was pressed tight to Menace. Their world went gray. Some animals were too stunned to move. Others crawled over dinosaur, carnivorous and other to live. Ape creatures took to the trees which did zero good. Only the thinking species or those animals capable of flight were safe, possibly.

The earth shook with the assault; some in the cave stumbled or were thrown to the ground. So much damage so fast came on deadly wings. The humans pressed back as boulders fell to cascade down the massive mountain. A cloud of black ash formed far to the left in the darkening sky. The sounds echoed in the ears of all as the earth screamed. Raw earth bubbled to the surface where it had lain dormant for a millennium. Exposed and new the sheer ancient aroma was an attack. Twisters formed as the rain flew up from the ground only to rain back down. There was a fight in the sky as clouds battled the earth for victory. Clouds accustomed to gathering the rain before releasing it exploded as the tsunami formed and raped the unsuspecting land.

The ground split apart across much of the region severing the continent into many. Humans were separated, many more died, and species were lost. Large chasms opened splitting the world. Solace watched as tiny ants below scrambled up the side of the mountain but it was too late. Their diversion worked. The hybrids faced numerous traps waiting. The traps hadn't been necessary. The pounding water flung their bodies in all directions. Solace was told a hybrid couldn't swim. Their bodies were too heavy. The hybrids lived inside smaller mountains, but their domiciles weren't high enough, their bodies washed out through cave openings.

As the water continued to rise those up high held their breath. The air was choking. The altitude too much for some added with thick clouds of ash. Water, putrid and smelling of decay, came down in gray sheets sending everyone deeper inside. The whipping wind howled through the icy caverns, voices of death, so it seemed. Weeping was heard. Many chose the arms of others to sob in.

"We are lost," Edge said as he held his mate.

"I am grateful Flight is with his father and safe, though my arms ache to hold the only child I will ever have," Aba said.

Others voiced similar thoughts of impending death. There was hopelessness etched on many faces. Rex buried his head under Luke's arm. The boy clung to Kiki who wrapped an open arm around the dog who scurried close. The twins were sobbing against Clarity's shoulder while Nina and Em sat with Nick. The young teen appeared horrified. They all were, none having been exposed to such disasters. Solace knew what was coming and hadn't been prepared.

"We are a strong people," Doom shouted. "We will persevere."

"We will all drown, there is nowhere higher to go unless we all want to freeze to death," Edge shouted.

"We have many furs and skins, we won't freeze if we need to go higher," Heath yelled.

Solace gazed over at the cowboy. She hadn't given him much thought while away. He was a gentle soul, somewhat decent with a sword, but he preferred peace. Heath went to take Em in his arms and tried to quiet the children as well as Nick.

Strong partitions were placed across the entryway, fastened high and hard to shield them, four double-sided furs of the mastodon hybrids they skinned were weighted down with boulders many men had moved attached to the large ivory tusks of furred beasts. Within the cave were natural lighted blue rocks, slabs of various sizes, some dusted in pure white snow crystals that made their way inside on breezes. The villagers moved back into the mountain with the many walls shielding them. If the water continued to rise they would drown. The partitions kept out the rain and ash, for now. If the need arose, they would slip deeper into the mountainside and higher, but had to be careful of earthquakes. Doom's village had never encountered the ground beneath their feet moving except for when the plane flew in from a sinkhole.

Menace took Solace to a fur, one of many spread on the cave floor. The air was cold the higher they ventured, it was now frigid. Torches were lit. Soon huge fires were blazing for warmth, they were safe from the prying eyes of the hybrids, and it didn't matter if they knew where they were. Solace doubted any survived the initial waves. If some made it higher up the mountain there would be few and the hunters were watchful arranging sentries. There would be no quarter given, there was to be no truce. All hybrids must be destroyed. If the hybrids made their way higher in their own homes they wouldn't have had a chance to grab provisions or fuel. Theirs would be a slow hungering and freezing death.

"You knew this was coming?" Menace said to Solace.

"I had an idea of what it would be like."

"I have never seen the likes of nature battling as we do with the hybrids. Only the blood is water; the waves weapons and winds slice as would swords. The clashing sounds are all around us. How long will we endure this?"

Solace gazed into his troubled eyes. "I don't know, my love. I do know we will endure."

The people couldn't battle the elements, but they prepared as best they could. While in hiding they drank cold water and ate traveling food. Now was the time for real sustenance. The villagers worked hard the previous weeks, all of them almost to complete exhaustion. Hot teas were prepared. Cheese was sliced and flatbread cooked. Children still needed to eat. Heath, six foot two, dark curly hair, brown-eyed stood with Luke and

Em. Solace rose and went to them by the fires that gave off not only warmth but light. The other children gathered and a few adults.

"Where are the other men, and Joey?" Nina asked. The children had been sequestered up the mountain for the long month before the meteor struck. "I thought maybe they came after the fight. Where are they?"

"Left behind?" Nick sneered.

Solace hadn't had much chance to converse with anyone other than the adults, Kiki and Luke. Nick had been traveling back and forth up the mountain, and she directly avoided Nick while busy. The teen was with them only because he believed what Solace said about needing to be on higher ground. Nick knew easier ways to travel up through the mountain. He proved to be an annoying boon.

"I was wondering when they'd show up myself," Lochlan said. "I hope they aren't on the other side of the planet."

Solace was certain the aliens thought all here were expendable. "I'm so sorry, Lochlan, we've been so busy and I should have told everyone day one what happened. The others, Tain and Bastian, went to another planet. Not by choice but they will be fine. Joe knows too much about flight. The alien let him keep his son knowing he would search again, forever if he had to. I think it was originally Joey Jr. they wanted."

"The others won't bother to come find me, even though we were together for almost a year. It was always Joey they were after, now they have him, thankfully," Lochlan said. "I came to call them friends. I wish them well wherever they ended up."

Solace placed her hand on his arm. "I think the

aliens were impressed with your fight aptitude and figured we could use all the help we can get. From what I saw when I got here they were right. Too bad you couldn't have brought a gun."

Lochlan gave her a cocky grin. "Being a badass is my specialty. Gun or not. Special forces."

"I thought there was some military in you. I never asked you before but are you from my Earth?" Solace asked.

"Not sure. Joe picked me up last. We ended up fighting back to back on a planet that didn't care much for humans. Their people were intelligent but thought we were barbarians. I suppose we were considering we had to shoot our way out. Ugly little dark purple things with mops of black hair and big yellow eyes. Half my size. They used telekinesis as their weapons. We were all immune, guess that's why they don't like humans. They think we have no brain so their weapons are useless. They learned how to dance a good jig when I shot at their hairy feet.

"I went through a sinkhole and ended up in hell. Their planet was fiery balls of meteors that flamed from all over. I think it's how they heat the planet. That and gas. I was pretty surprised when Joe fueled the plane while Bastian, Tain and I kept the beings at bay. Little buggers were none too happy with us stealing their fuel. Then we took off, fast."

"Do you have this mark?" Solace showed him her inoculation. It was the only way they could tell the humans apart. Heath didn't have the mark and was from a docile planet. So were a few other children. Kiki, Luke, Nina, Em, and the twins were from Solace and Clarity's Earth. So had been Joey Jr.

"Yep, I got one of those marks," Lochlan concurred. Solace thought so. The way he fought was nowhere near docile.

Ladles of soup were given out in bowls from dug trenches covered in bones while hot coals burned beneath. The laid bones kept the hides from scorching both inside and out when burning stones were added to aid in the heating. A small amount of liquid seeped through to keep the flames from scorching it. A rough hide was spread overtop to cook their meal, hung from large antler bones. It was a somber dinner while the mountain whistled and shook. Bubble-gum and Rex weren't huge eaters, it was the bulwarks and cave hyena that caused most of the worries. Large caverns higher up were frozen and filled with large whole animals or haunches of meat. For now the beasts took their kills, minus the hides, deeper into caverns to gorge alone. Once finished they wouldn't need to eat for a week, or more depending on their restricted activity. If the animals could sleep they wouldn't need to feed for some time.

The hunters had been busier than ever the last week collecting as many animals as possible. Many mastodon mammoth hybrids were stockpiled in manageable pieces. Others built their traps on the ground trying to be unobtrusive yet not wanting the hybrids to think nothing was amiss. Many more gathered edible plant life while secretly scurrying their supplies to higher ground. Everything edible was carried from their domed homes to the mountaintop. There were enough provisions to last many months if necessary. There were furs piled high for warmth and all burnable fuel was collected. They needed to ride out the storms with as much room as needed for the large village in as little space as possible. They were able to spread out to connecting caverns but that would burn necessary fuel faster.

In the distance Solace noted fires from other mountains. Between them was a chasm of endless sea. She wondered how other villages faired. Menace came to her and led her back to a deep impression in the ground piled high first with straw then furs. There were many of the beds scattered around. The children liked to group together near the bustle of activity where adults were closer.

Many of the villagers were terrified. They'd never seen the weather so disagreeable. The skies never before filled with foul ash. The earth didn't burp and temper tantrum. Solace knew it could be much worse. They were on the other side of where the meteor hit, those in its path were incinerated. The cold weather came fast and black snowflakes were seen through cracks in the hides. She knew the boundaries of the continent now *continents* were being determined. She hoped blistering heat hadn't fried others as the continents split.

That night she lay pressed tight to Menace listening to nature's sounds of hell. "There is something I need to tell you."

Menace pressed a lock of her hair behind her ear. "You are so beautifully radiant."

"I'm pregnant."

His eyes grew round and his stunned expression would have been amusing if not for the seriousness of their situation. Solace found herself crushed to his chest. When she gazed up at him he was smiling, and he was sobbing, though no tears fell.

"I'm so sorry you are in danger with our child my love."

"I knew I was pregnant before I came back to this planet. You know the alien brought me to him as you battled. What I didn't tell you was I was given a choice, to go somewhere safe or to come back take my chances and warn everyone."

"You could have been safe?"

"I could have been alone without you."

"Do you love me that much?"

Solace smiled. "How much is *that* much?"

"For me it is keeping me in your heart. If your heart stops beating mine will too. If you no longer breathe I will cease to exist. Our child is within you as well. Are you feeling very crowded?"

She was about to laugh but saw he was serious. "Ask me that again in a few months."

"This child of ours should have a name."

"We don't know if it's a boy or a girl."

"We must think about names for both." Menace lay back with an arm under his head.

High winds rattled the partitions sounding as though skeletons were dancing. Solace couldn't see the barriers from behind the thick cave wall their bedding was protected from and Menace didn't notice. She could see he was thinking of nothing else but the baby. The water outside ceased to rise higher but had yet to abate, the waves rolling and crashing in the high winds. A tiny T-rex waved at her when she noticed him. Rex's arms, not as short as his ancestors, were still tiny. The dinosaur went back to licking a soup bowl. Luke tried to take it from him when Rex bit the bowl and a game of tug of war ensued. Child and dino took turns at flinging each other around causing a tiny stir of smiles. The cave hyena that roamed in and flopped by Kiki farted causing those around to scoot away, and Kiki waved a hand in front of her face shoving at the massive beast in disgust.

"Go back to your food you smelly old thing," Kiki grouched.

Bongo yawned, farted again, and settled. Bubblegum played dead, his tongue lolling out the side of his mouth. Em and Nina groaned dramatically. Blue pulled the dogs tail worried he was in fact dead. The dog farted and Solace would have sworn he smiled. Blue fell back into Cole bellowing. Solace was in comical horror hell. Menace didn't move, eyes trained on the ceiling above. Across from her Doom wrinkled his nose and glared at Clarity who was the one who insisted the animals were family and needed to be with them.

"Well?" Solace finally asked Menace.

"This will take thought," Menace replied. "Doom was an appropriate name. His father thought the villages were doomed, but it appears it is the hybrids who were doomed. My father named me Menace. A hard warrior who would rise from adversity to be a menace to his own people so they would die."

"Oh, Menace. Is that what you thought?"

"I wandered endlessly thinking they died and it was because I had grown into my name."

"My mother named me Solace to give my father peace in a world that could be filled with war and hate and anger. No matter where he went he could always find solace. Me."

"Perhaps Clarity is perspective."

Solace settled beside him thinking he was right. Their child needed a perfect name for a new beginning. Something to lead them into the future. She yawned thinking she was so damned tired all the time. If the world was going to end she couldn't stop it. She pressed close to Menace. All she had was now.

****

Menace stood outside the cave past the partitions. Doom joined him. Water stretched for miles. Carcasses and debris floated in crashing waves. The ash covered the sun and Menace shivered from cold. Their lush planet was damned.

"Solace says if the ash remains we need to leave. We need to find sun or we will die when our food runs out," Menace said.

"Clarity says the same. It would be impossible right now with the water so high. I never imagined this. Clarity tried to explain but I honestly thought she was exaggerating. This is nothing I've encountered. We are lucky we made the high covering partitions with small holes to filter the air. Or we would be covered in ash inside. Breathing would be unbearable. As I stand here I can feel my lungs protest."

"Do you think this will pass, this destruction?"

"Yes."

The earth trembled beneath them, shaking as though frightened or cold. Menace thought of creatures with life, vegetation with life, but to think of the earth with life was a different concept to him. He wondered why he hadn't put his ideas together before. The earth was alive to give birth to life. Was it afraid? The life-giving water attacked the land. Menace could see cracks in the mountain, deep holes. Had the earth fought and lost? It was wounded. Menace touched a huge boulder filled with compassion.

"Do not fear. Your humans will continue to respect you. We will continue to appreciate your bounty and generosity. We thank you for allowing us to partake of your beauty." Then to Doom, "I think our planet is hiding, afraid it will be hurt again."

"Perhaps. I never thought such destruction was possible. I never knew a planet could be so cruel to itself. I would not rip off my flesh, or cut a deep hole within. I would not rage with the wind."

"But we do," Menace said filled with wonder. "When we are hurt we bleed. We rage when angry. Our emotions tear us apart, and our love creates life. Solace grows life within."

"That's wonderful," Doom clapped him on the back.

"I only hope the planet understands what happens is beyond its control. If I can be fixed by love I think the planet can. If the water recedes the lands will forgive the intrusion. The holes and cracks can be considered character marks. There will always be battle wounds, scars, but we all carry them."

Doom gazed at the tattoos visible on Menace, and Menace chose not to hide them.

"The marks are not yours my friend."

"Then who do they belong to?"

"The wind."

"The wind, eh?" Menace raised an eyebrow. "With the way that damned hyena farts, the tattoos should have been blasted into the tornado."

Doom chuckled and Solace appeared holding two steaming cups. "Clarity wants to see you, Doom."

Doom left them alone and Solace gave a delectable meaty-smelling broth to Menace. He took a sip and closed his eyes. The flavor, thick and filling rolled down his throat to heat his insides. He was happy to be home on his planet. He would be happier to have Solace beneath him in his own domicile with the world the way it was before. The wind whipped Solace's hair around her face, and she battled to keep strands from her lips as she sipped from her cup. She tugged the fur around her shoulders tighter.

"You should be in by the fire," he said.

"I wanted to be alone with you. You should at least put a fur around you. It's cold."

"I don't want my tattoos covered for any length of time. The sacrifices should see what I do and know I keep them safe."

She was quiet for a moment. "I know you carry a great burden, but it's not yours, not really. The aliens are keeping those souls safe with you until they can be set free somewhere else."

"Until that day comes, they are my responsibility."

Solace settled onto a rock and stared below. Lightning zipped across the water, and the water crackled. Above clouds groaned, too full to accept any more moisture. Then to Menace's surprise it began to rain. Huge ugly drops landed on him, zigzagging a dirty trail across his chest, and he gazed up.

"That's odd. Normally the rain begins from ground up, then down to saturate everything."

"I think many things are going to change on your planet. Let's hope there is no ice age and let's hope this gray rain clears." She scooted farther under an overhang holding an open hand over the opening of the steaming mug in her hand.

"Did a meteor bounce off your planet?"

"Nope, smacked it silly. Wiped out around seventy-five percent of all living things millions of years ago, maybe sixty-five million."

"Then we should be fine. We were, uh, pushed not smacked."

"Clarity and I have been speculating. We think your planet now has continents; oceans could separate you from others. If that's true there may still be hybrids. Instead of space flight they'll need to make boats. Either way we might be looking at hundreds of years of growth from both sides."

"We will be ready."

Solace chuckled. "Our children's children will be. We can make certain. Between Lochlan, Clarity and I we can make guns. You never mentioned what happened on that planet with the hybrid."

"The hybrid is dead and the plane was destroyed. I wished for you. When the sinkhole opened and swallowed me I wanted to slide into your arms. Imagine my surprise when my first involuntary cuddle came from Doom."

"I landed on Muffin." Solace laughed and Menace grinned.

Menace drained his cup setting it onto the boulder and pulled her into his arms. He kissed her. She collapsed against his chest and he lifted her to cuddle. He encouraged her to drink her breakfast; their little one would need sustenance to grow. She should be warmed. The rain came down harder, and Menace took her inside. Who knew how long they would be trapped? While trapped, it was important to keep up spirits. He led Solace to a hide filled with more steaming broth and made certain she drank more. He wasn't certain how much she should eat but something told him he would need to watch her carefully. She was the kind of female who would give away her last mouthful to another. The way the T-rex was lapping at another bowl of stew chances were the dinosaur would be the first.

Chapter Eleven

The water's retreat was slow at first then gained momentum as time passed in exaggerated slowness, the ground was taking back its territory an inch at a time. Thankfully, most of the debris was pulled back, and the tide took the bodies of many species with it. The skies remained dull. The rain was black and unpalatable. The villagers were saved from dehydration by the accumulation of ice kept safe inside the caves. They could hack off clean chunks and warm them. Being high above many clouds the snow was clear when parties ventured higher. They didn't often as air was dense and the altitude frigid.

Inside the caves, people worked leather hides to keep busy, and they were down to two meals a day. Menace stared often past the partitions that had seen better days and were in constant need of repair. Solace was recovering from a bout of illness. She claimed it was normal but Menace worried, never having seen a pregnant female. She stayed in her furs much of the day while the women fussed over her, thinking her delicate. Solace didn't correct them; she wanted to wait until the first few months passed before telling everyone their news. Only Doom and Clarity knew she was pregnant.

"How are you feeling?" Menace asked her when he returned to their furs.

"Lazy." She yawned and stretched.

"Are you hungry?"

She grimaced. "I don't suppose you could find me some hotdogs and vanilla ice cream?" She then chuckled at his puzzled look. "I'm guessing no."

"There is flatbread. Kiki stuffs chunks of meat into it with cheese and sometimes leafy greens. The children like it."

"How are the supplies?"

"Let me worry about that."

"I'm not an invalid."

"You are creating life. You work at it day and night. It must be exhausting to never have your body rest." He pulled her to his chest and placed a hand onto her belly. "Inside of you we both grow. You and I joined to make a child, a you-me, or a me-you. I do live inside of you. You have no other responsibility but to nurture the life within you. You are so lucky."

"Yes the privilege of puking and bloating is mine."

Menace was concerned. "Don't you want our baby?"

"Of course I do. I'm moody."

He laughed then lowered his voice. "There is a child inside of you. Of course you're moody, have you seen the way children behave? My poor love you can't leave the room from this baby and take a breath to clear your head. You cannot say hush now or shut up, like you do to Rex. There is no quieting the one inside and you, my love, are the only one who knows how you feel."

"I guess I do feel a little hungry."

The petulance in her tone made him grin. "I will make you a Kiki sandwich."

"No ketchup."

He grimaced as he rose to his feet. Ketchup, the blood of the undead. No wonder the children in the cave loved it; they acted like demon spawns most days. They needed to be outside running in fresh air, not cooped up smelling cave hyena farts.

****

Menace, Doom, Edge and Lochlan were the first to venture out after a bulwark returned with a fresh kill, a young mastodon hybrid. The villagers took a share of the meat and left the bulwark to fend off the other animals. Fortified with fresh meat, the four trudged for days down the side of the mountain.

Their underground homes were intact. There was no water damage. Inside was dry but the air was stale. It was surreal to walk their homes when no other was around. No children tussling with animals, no females cooking and gossiping. No bombs made or swords forged. The four sat at a table and ate a small meal.

"It's so quiet," Menace said.

"I feel like a ghost in my own home," Edge said.

"It will be better when we're all together," Doom said.

"I wouldn't mind seeing that little T-rex running around sticking his tongue out at me," Lochlan said and laughed. "But I sure as hell don't miss the hyena's ass."

"Let's get out of here." Talk of homemade Menace worry for Solace.

The surrounding ground was squishy. They decided a few more days inside the mountain was necessary. There was a small glimpse of the sun trying to break free. Much of the foliage was dead. What was left was drooping or wilted. The ocean had left a few unusual items. Giant clams and oysters were pried open.

"Fuck me, look at this," Lochlan exclaimed. He held up a huge round ball.

"What is it?" Menace asked.

"A pearl."

"Can you eat it?" Doom asked.

"No," Lochlan said and gave him a sheepish grin. "I guess it's pretty worthless here but the meat might be good if it hasn't spoiled." He dropped the pearl to bounce near the shell it came from.

The noise startled a pair of velociraptors who were creeping close, but Menace noted it wasn't in a hostile way. The male was supporting the female, or rather they were supporting each other. They were wounded. There was no blood but bruising could be seen. Doom drew his sword but Menace stopped him and pointed. Two young ones hid in a bush. The little ones were small, thin, and needed food.

"Enough death," Menace said. "Besides, if we kill the adults, we can't leave the little ones to fend for themselves, and we'll be adding baby raptors to our growing list of animal pets. Can you imagine the names Clarity would think up for these two?"

Doom groaned. "Something along the lines of Cotton and Kitty, no doubt."

"Oh no, I'm certain Clarity will name them something sickly sweet. I ain't running around a cave calling out for Pampered and Precious to come eat," Lochlan grouched.

The others chuckled and Menace took his pack off his back and pulled out a huge piece of meat Solace packed for him. All four raptors gazed in hunger. The little ones chirped and slinked through their parents' legs in eager excitement. Using a sharp knife, he cut the meat into sections, he tossed the smaller bits to the little ones and larger chunks to the adults. Menace heard Doom sigh and he did the same. There was enough bread cooked and broth in skins to eat on the way back. They hollowed out the rest of a massive tree trunk that was already showing signs of age. They lined the damp bottom with dried branches. The raptors took shelter and were given more food. The hunters covered the trunk completely from view, allowing the small family to sleep and stay warm.

"That may come back to bite us in the ass," Doom said.

"Literally." Lochlan snorted.

"I'm so sick of the death. I know we will have to hunt again, but we have enough food for some time and did you see there are beasts that made it up the mountain after all. There were mastodon mammoths. They might have finally figured out what we were trying to tell them," Menace said.

"Menace am I mistaken or have you gone from badass to mommy dearest? Before, it was 'kill the fuckers.' Now we may as well make you a wreath for your head with roses. What's up? Solace seems to be having a lot of 'morning' sickness," Lochlan said.

"Menace has discovered he's going to be a father," Doom said and grinned.

"Solace didn't want to tell anyone yet," Menace said with annoyance.

"Wonderful," Edge grouched. "One look at a baby and every female will want one including Aba."

"Don't be annoyed, Menace," Lochlan said. "I've seen a few pregnant women in my time and guessed a while ago. I'm surprised no one else has."

"We haven't been around pregnant females," Doom reminded him. "I was the last born to my village. Menace was the last born to his."

Lochlan gazed around. "If there will be babies born we'll need to make certain we can find more food."

"If the hybrids are gone or their numbers greatly reduced we could do some growing," Menace said. "The planet Solace, Lochlan and I were on kept these funny looking things called goats, or were they sheep or was it mouflon? Anyway, imagine having food so close you could walk into a corral and pick up dinner. The meat is convenient, right at their fingertips, and not too large to be uncontrollable. With milk as well and cheese and butter they make."

"Ah the beginning of fast food has started," Lochlan said. "Mouflon nuggets. We could start a franchise."

Menace had no clue what the man was talking about. He was anxious to get back to Solace. The closer to the mountain the ground was squishier. Inland had been less wet but the damage was significant, the ocean appeared closer. It took a few days to climb the mountain with its intricate turns. They were hungry when they finally returned. The familiar smells of home invaded his nostrils leading them the last few feet as tummies rumbled.

"You're back," Solace cried, and raced into his arms.

Everyone was anxious. They waited for Doom to speak and gathered close. Blue demanded Menace pick him up. He reached for both twins while encircling Solace. In a way Menace realized the twins were like his own, no one laid claim to them, they seemed to lay claim to him and Solace.

"We can go home soon," Doom said. "The water is retreating but the animals have suffered a great deal. This may prove to be a hard winter. I know summer is here but the vegetation has drowned. Plant life will come back eventually but maybe not until next year. Once we come down from the mountain we might need a discussion on if we should leave."

Concerned voices followed. "The deep sleep will come. We must return before the hibernation," Edge said. More of the same comments followed, all fearful and high-pitched.

"I agree," Doom shouted above the din. "But until then we might need to migrate farther afield, hunt, forage, and then return with our bounty."

"But how will we make our cheese?" Aba asked. "Our fermented drinks?"

"The village was so full of food last year I shudder to think what we'll need to carry back," Heath said.

"We didn't survive the hybrids to die now," Menace yelled, he placed the boys on their feet next to Solace and went to stand with Doom.

"It's safe here," Solace said. "Why not send out hunting and gathering parties for now?"

"They might have to travel very far, hiking up and down the mountain is difficult and time consuming," Doom said. "There will be many dangers."

"And there weren't before?" was Edge's sarcastic response.

Menace and Doom gazed at each other and shrugged. "For now let's eat and rest," Menace said.

****

Solace lay back on the fur. She waited for Menace to come to bed. When he climbed in beside her she reached for him.

"You're naked; you'll freeze," Menace said and gathered her close while piling more furs on her.

"Your baby is a furnace, besides you can keep me warm."

Menace rolled onto her but kept his weight from her. "You didn't light the overhead torch."

"Thankfully my need to pee every five minutes has passed. I don't need the light anymore. I'm more interested in privacy."

Solace cupped the back of his head to pull him closer. She tasted his lips. Soft, full and firm, his mouth was heaven. She heard him groan and the stiff erection near her waist made her smile.

"You should be naked, too," she said.

Menace shifted, pulling the furs up over their heads. Solace helped him guide his hide pants off. He had reverted to the same booties he was used to, while Solace refused to give up the stylish ones made for her on the ancient planet of All People. She tried not to giggle as he pulled the leather from his feet remembering Clarity called Doom 'booty boy' on occasion.

When Menace settled down, he stretched out beside her. He lifted his hand to smooth the hair from her face. It was light enough to vaguely make out the outline of his jaw.

"Some of the others know you carry our child," he said.

"I suppose it won't hurt to tell the rest."

"We are hunting tomorrow. Others scouted and

saw tracks. If we are successful we can have a feast."

"I hope there is other life out there."

"There is. Some. We will make a home for our family."

"You are my home."

"And you are mine."

This time when Menace kissed her the tingle he stirred went straight to her heat making her sizzle.

"I need you," she whispered.

"I have to make you ready."

"I am."

Solace spread her legs and pushed her hips under him. Cautiously Menace tested her depth with two fingers.

"See I told you," she said and panted.

His perfectly hard hot cock stroked into her making her gasp in delight. His arms were bent at her shoulders only allowing the tips of her nipples to touch his chest. His movement tickled them. She nipped at his throat when he plunged down. Sliding up she gripped his powerful arms.

"Harder, Menace."

"Softer," he teased.

He moved slower. Solace gritted her teeth. They should be bouncing all over the cave with her need. She pulled her legs up to wrap around his waist. She encouraged him with squeezes to pump harder. The sweat formed at her temples and she could feel a drop slide down. Finally Menace complied and her body jerked when his cock plunged hard.

"I love you," Solace said on a hard whisper.

Waves of pleasure washed over her when he thumped against her three more times. Menace growled his release. His breathing was heavy when he rolled to the side taking her with him. He gripped her tight as though loath to release her. His lips were at her ear.

"Thank you, Solace. Thank you for loving me. Thank you for carrying our baby. Whatever you need me to do to make you comfortable just ask. You are creating a human inside you. You are working every day. If you needed me to carry you everywhere I would."

"Sometimes I forget you have never seen a pregnant female. I couldn't ask for a better mate and this baby could never have a better father."

Menace kissed her forehead. She snuggled into his warmth enjoying the feel of his warm skin against hers.

****

A hunting and gathering party formed in the early morning. The trail down the mountain was tedious and took a number of days with the added females. Menace made certain to watch Solace for any sign of aches or tiredness. She seemed in a fine mood which made him happy and relieved. Once down the mountain the two groups split to cover more ground. Doom, Clarity, Menace, Solace, and Lochlan made up one group, followed closely by Kiki, Luke, Rex, Bongo, and Muffin. They were in search of not only game but also the few cow seal-like creatures who gave milk for cheese in exchange for safety from other predators. If they came across the beasts, they would send Muffin back for a third group.

The remainder of the village stayed put to protect their supplies and children. Bubble-gum was left to watch over the rambunctious twins. Three other bulwarks kept guard. The beasts were allowed to go free one at a time to hunt for their own food. Wood was collected and dried as needed.

As Menace neared a hollowed tree a velociraptor came forward teeth snapping. Muffin was ready to take up the attack but was stopped. Menace held out his hands in supplication and approached with caution. He lowered the pack he carried. The raptor didn't strike, but held back. Two little heads peeked out the tree trunk. They were less reserved and raced forward to yank at Menace's pant leg. The adult raptor shook his head in what appeared to be annoyance.

Menace reached to stroke each little head then handed the little ones a sizable chunk of meat. They retreated back into their home.

"On no, look," Solace said and pointed.

The female raptor was slouched, an arm dangling. She was thinner.

"It's broken," Clarity said. "She must be in a lot of pain."

Clarity inched off her pack and sprinkled a chunk of meat with a powdery substance. She tossed the meat to the female. The raptor nudged the food then ate with tiny bites. She whistle whimpered while she ate.

"That's it girl, eat up," Clarity said.

Solace gazed at Clarity with a grin. "Well you can't do this alone."

"What are you two planning?" Menace asked.

"Keep the dad busy," Clarity said.

The female was slouched. Solace grabbed a few flat branches and pounded any slivers off. Menace groaned when the women approached the female. The male called a warning and Menace stepped forward with a chunk of meat. He sliced pieces and tossed them to the male one at a time. The male ate but kept a wary eye on the women. Clarity straightened the arm with Solace's aid, and they proceeded to splint the raptor's arm, then wrapped everything in a tight hide. They left more meat and moved on.

"First aid on a dinosaur, a raptor," Luke said while shaking his head. The T-rex beside him nudged his head under the boy's arm. "Well, don't be upset. I found you as an egg. You were pretty boring to look at. Now you're cute."

The devastation surrounding them went on for miles. Many huge trees still stood but were recovering from a near drowning experience. The air was different somehow when Menace breathed in. It was much like the scent of losing his people—loss. The earth was grieving. If the planet were female Menace could picture a naked battered and bruised woman cold, soaked and clinging to a large rock, head bowed in defeat, weeping. His heart hurt with the image.

"Will we be all right?" Kiki asked in a quiet voice.

Clarity put her arm around her. "Yes."

"Everything looks power washed," Luke grumbled.

"I can't believe you remembered Daddy using the power wash," Kiki said.

"I remember the sound of the water and the blast it caused when it hit the siding on our house." Luke ducked his head then gazed at his sister. "I don't remember what our parents looked like."

Kiki hugged him then slung and arm around his neck in mock play while Luke struggled to free himself. Rex squealed and raced to Luke's aid but a hyena blocked the way.

"I'm gonna let Rex lick your bowl," Luke yelled.

"Then I'll make sure Bongo farts on your furs before bed," Kiki taunted.

"Ew, no not that," Solace said. "We finally have him sticking his ass out the cave door."

Kiki laughed and shoved Luke away. Rex stuck his tongue out at her. For miles they traveled searching for salvation. The jungle grew thicker then came to a clearing. The mammoth mastodons they came across brought relief. There were ten in the herd. All were bathing in a clear pond or rolling in the sandy dirt beside the water's edge. One nursed her young.

"Damn I wish I had my gun," Lochlan said.

"We all wish we had your gun," Menace retorted.

"A gun?" Doom asked.

"The weapon Clarity told us about, it's real and kickass."

"Solace do you have those blue numbing rocks?" Menace asked.

She held up a wooden tube filled with rocks and sand. "How many do you need?" she asked.

Menace took the container and gave her a hard stare. "I'll let you know once we've downed a beast."

"I thought I was out here to hunt," she said in annoyance.

Lochlan chuckled. "Silly girl, you're out here for him to keep an eye on you."

"Kiki and Luke go be annoying," Doom said.

With a whoop the two took off followed by the T-rex. Muffin and the hyena were a danger to the beasts and stalked off to get behind them on the other side of the small pond. Menace climbed a tree after making certain Solace was in a safe place. He could see Doom and Clarity getting into position. The children were harassing one young cow. Menace chuckled at the faces Luke made by sticking out his tongue and pulling his mouth wide with his fingers. The cow snorted not sure what to make of the tiny little being.

The monarch of the group went after Rex making the little dinosaur squeal in terror and run around the herd waving little arms in the air. While the leader was busy, Kiki added her harassing calls to the same cow as Luke. The young cow became separated from the herd in the confusion. It was then Muffin and Bongo raced from hiding; the shallow water did nothing to hinder their mad dash. The sound of the spraying water startled the herd. The matriarch realized the deception too late. Her bugled call to run was answered by all but one. The lone cow ran in a different direction now followed by Doom and Clarity. Lochlan stood whooping and hollering when the cow tried to bank right. She couldn't go back, and she couldn't go left or right. Her only opening was straight ahead toward the jungle.

Fast outdistancing the others in her terror, the cow ran under the tree Menace was hiding in and he dumped the entire container, sand and blue rocks, onto the beast. The reaction was almost instantaneous. She dropped, incapacitated. Menace leaped onto her back and slit her throat. The blue rocks were carefully collected back into the container with sand, extracted from the cow without being touched. They worked fast cutting the meat, worried about other predators, but the surrounding area was oddly quiet. With one exception.

The male raptor approached with hesitance, head bowed in deference, limping. He'd followed them. The dinosaur was almost as thin as his mate, and it was apparent the food he caught wasn't much, and most was given to the offspring. After removing the hide of their kill, Menace hacked off an entire leg and dragged it toward the raptor. The raptor eyed him and the meat.

"Do not get used to this," Menace said as he turned and walked away.

"Watch out," Doom yelled.

The raptor was on Menace. Arms and legs wrapped around him, cheek to cheek. A wet tongue licked his face and he groaned. The raptor released him and hobbled back to the leg bone covered in meat to drag it off for his family. Menace wiped a hand across his sloppy wet cheek.

"Ew."

"Menace has a new love," Luke taunted. "Hope Solace don't get mad."

"Very funny," Menace said with a growl to the boy who danced away howling with laughter, a chuckling T-rex went with him.

"We may as well set up right here," Doom said.

"We can make a number of huge fires and once the meat is dry send it in packs on Muffin and Bongo back to the caves," Solace said. "In fact, if we send a huge raw load now they may send more people to help cut it up. Muffin can scale that mountain in less than a day."

"Good idea," Menace said.

"Are you sure she won't eat it?" Lochlan asked.

Menace smiled. "No. She's a good girl and knows we won't let her starve. She's very loyal and listens well. Same with Kiki's hyena if she's the one to ask. That beast will do anything for Kiki."

They soon had a few solid haunches of raw meat packed onto the large bulwark wrapped in hides. With a slap to her rump Muffin took off at a run. The hyena was next following hot on Muffin's heels with his own load after a few sweet words from his master and beloved friend.

Solace was gazing after the bulwark. "She is getting bigger. I wonder how soon before she has her cubs."

"I have no clue," Clarity said. "But if the males kill the offspring of cubs not their own we'll be in for trouble. Those cubs are Bubble-gum's. He can't defend the litter from the bulwark males."

"Then, we will," Menace said. He winked at Solace who seemed worried. "Nothing will dare harm any cub born to us again."

She smiled and he went back to butchering the animal.

****

They came equipped with a large hide tent but all preferred to sleep close to the fires. Sleeping outdoors was a novelty for Doom and Menace. With so few carnivores in the area there was little to fear. There wasn't a brontosaur in sight to risk a stampede. Each man paced while keeping a close watch as the sky darkened. Solace was sitting on a sleeping fur next to Clarity.

"Clarity, do you think the earth was formed when aliens played pool?"

Clarity laughed. "I'm inclined to believe anything."

Solace studied the beautiful woman with mid length blonde hair that was almost white. A contrast to Solace's dark locks. She never imagined she would become fast friends in a primal world with another of her own world. They had known each other for only a year and yet Solace could tell Clarity anything.

"The alien almost didn't let me return," Solace said.

"He didn't let me at all," Clarity said. "I knew I had to get away. I'm surprised you have no tracking devise."

"Do you?"

"Not anymore. It was ripped out very unpleasantly after the alien brought Doom back to life. He said there would be no more interference but I guess he meant with me."

"Menace envies Doom's unmarred skin."

"Remember, Doom paid for the release of those victims with his life."

"The alien said our DNA, our blood type specifically shouldn't be here," Solace said, her hand to her belly.

"Are you afraid the aliens will take your baby?"

"A little."

"We won't let that happen."

Clarity hugged her and rolled over. It had been a long day and Solace was exhausted. Sleep wouldn't come. She glanced over at Kiki and Luke. Rex curled up beside the boy. Solace smiled when the boy rolled taking the cover exposing the dinosaur flesh to the cool night air. The T-rex shivered, grabbed a corner, and rolled taking the fur with him. The boy shivered and the action was repeated until Solace rose and draped a fur over the tiny dinosaur, then returned to her bed. In the distance she saw the approach of Muffin and Bongo. The cave hyena dropped beside Kiki and yawned. Kiki cuddled closer to the huge beast. Muffin went to Clarity and was soon settled between the women, the beast certainly had the wolverine stamina, but her exhaustion was apparent. Muffin and Bongo must have raced the entire way there and back. The bulwark was a furnace, her fur, neither too rough nor soft was a comfort pressed against her side.

Solace locked her fingers under her neck as she lay back, and gazed up at the few stars. There were night sounds emanating from various places. Not too far away Lochlan was snoring. Or perhaps it was Rex. The soft sound of the pacing men's *booties* made her smile at the word Clarity always used. A small breeze was chased by a bigger one, but the bulwark was a barrier. Her thoughts wandered. *Earth is billions of years old. Why are we, humans, given only a hundred years as certain species or less and why are certain species given longer? How long before another ice age on earth, her planet?*

She sighed realizing her Earth was a memory. So were the children lost to her. It was a comfort knowing they were okay. She could let go of her guilt; it wasn't hers to carry. The idea made her think of Menace and his tattoos. Would he be as lucky as Doom to be rid of the burden he carried? Then she remembered Doom died to be free of his. Solace shuddered. She lay awake until Menace crawled up beside her. His arms were warm and she finally found sleep when he kissed her forehead in a tender familiar gesture.

Chapter Twelve

The tantalizing aroma of meat woke Solace. She stretched and yawned. She had slept late. Muffin was beside her. She sat up and noted the bulwark was awake and keeping watch over her. Solace hugged the beast.

"Two pregnant ladies basking in the warm sunshine."

It was nice to see the sun again and to have heat tickle her skin. As a dark cloud floated overhead she frowned. The bulwark growled low in her throat. Muffin was soon up and snapping and snarling. A young hybrid was creeping toward the beast they'd felled the day before. They began the drying process of some. Solace was about to call to Menace but he had already seen the Neandersauri. It was apparent the young one wanted food.

Both Menace and Doom approached, swords drawn. The Neandersauri growled, whistled, and motioned angrily. His actions were haughty. He was the superior and the paltry humans must back away from the kill until he took his fill. Menace stepped forward. Solace was also on her feet and settled an arm over Muffin's furry neck. The hybrid hissed and lunged for Menace. Dropping low Menace sliced the legs off the creature. Solace put a hand to her mouth gagging. She was shocked. Menace normally aimed for a fast kill. The hybrid screamed as it dropped. Menace stood and strolled over. He stared back into the line of a wooded glen.

Solace and Doom followed his gaze. She could see other hybrids. With deliberation Menace lift the sword high and smashed the blade into the Hybrid's chest, and twisted. As he removed the weapon nine more hybrids burst forward. All young but as tall as she. Solace raced for her weapon. The bulwark was on the move and grabbed an enemy by the throat. A fast shake of her head, she severed an artery, blood spurt.

Kiki and Luke, back to back with a hyena and mini T-rex for support battled. Weapons were swung with tact, perfected aim was theirs. The hybrid went down. Clarity was battling alone and Solace raced to help her while Doom fought two. Lochlan went back and forth, his sword high then low to ward off wicked claws. The hybrids were young but dangerous slicing at them with huge claws.

Menace battled two near the body of the fallen Neandersauri. It seemed the hybrids were capable of feeling compassion for their own and she caught a few word whistles of rage. The battle was violent. Down went another hybrid. As she reached Clarity, Solace saw four more hybrids approach.

"Menace," she screamed. "There's more."

The hybrid who fought Clarity disarmed her, but instead of killing her, he grabbed her and tossed her over a shoulder. Solace couldn't run him through, she was afraid of killing Clarity.

"Doom," Clarity yelled as she beat at the hybrids back.

Doom slaughtered a hybrid but was fighting two more. Solace realized the goal wasn't the meat. It was a trick. They sent in one to see their actual number, to see if more humans were hiding. Once they realized they were alone the hybrids struck. Solace gagged as she ran for Clarity, knowing what must be done. She skid along the ground and swung hard severing the hybrid's legs at the calf. The pair flopped in a heap. Solace was up. As the hybrid swung wildly Solace cut his wrists. Hands fell to the ground.

A loud roar sounded and Solace placed a hand to her heart when she saw Edge and others from their village running to join the fight The gatherers had come to help with the meat, having seen the hyena and bulwark loaded with food from a distance and instead found a battle. The hybrids tried to retreat but there was no quarter. They were all killed. The fight was over and Solace was in Menace's arms.

Clarity, wrapped in Doom's embrace walked forward. "Thank you."

Solace gazed up at Menace. "He taught me that move."

Menace smiled. "I don't like for anything to suffer, but there are times when you must make an exception. I learned that on the last planet."

"I was wondering," Doom said. "Why you didn't just kill the hybrid."

"Those hybrids need to know we will show no mercy. If any are watching, and I think there are, they know we're done being subservient. No matter what, we will never bow to their needs again."

"Well now that everyone is here let's get this food back to our cave and have a celebration," Doom said.

"We are due a celebration," Edge said. "We found enough plant life to sustain us for a while. It's time we give ourselves some praise for beating the odds. Life will continue."

Menace gripped Solace close. "It certainly will."

****

They were weary as darkness fell. The hunters and the gatherers were successful. Bongo padded along with Luke and a package of meat draped over his back. Rex was dragging and making whining noises. Menace relieved the little dinosaur of his load. Every part of the mammoth mastodon was brought back, including tusks and bones. It was an exhausted lot who dropped onto furs after handing off their loads a few days later. The hyena flopped to the ground with a huge groan and fell asleep with Luke still on him.

"You look tired," Nick said to Kiki.

"We were attacked by hybrids and had to keep watch while we kept moving. We did have to sleep sometime. Mostly we were on the move. I need to rest."

The young woman, as Menace thought of her, closed her eyes. Solace refused to ride Muffin during their fast return, claiming the pregnant bulwark was needed as a guard. Neither Solace nor Muffin held a load of meat, Menace doubled up, as did Doom. Others made slings to carry huge amounts of food between them. Some pulled loads behind them strapped onto sturdy logs, the top each held in a hand, the bottom poles dragging along the ground. Their kill would feed the villagers for a while.

"I think it's time to introduce you people to the wheel," Clarity said and slumped onto a fur.

"A wagon would have been useful," Solace said.

Menace brought Solace meat and cooked plants. There were fresh roots and tubers. A hot thin gruel was bubbling over a fire. What the hunters needed was to crawl into their furs. Menace didn't remember ever being so tired. He worried about Solace. She ate, mechanically chewing her food. Menace knew if it weren't for the baby she'd lay back and close her eyes without eating. After a few bites she succumbed to slumber.

A storm that trailed them through the outskirts of open caverns, brought a rumbling wrath. The skies growled and snarled. The villagers were wary now that they knew some hybrids survived. There would need to be a constant watch. Returning to their domed homes was paramount but not until they were certain the waters retreated for good.

Menace lifted a hand to brush a lock of hair from Solace's face. He wanted more than anything to take her to their own bed in their homes below. To pamper her, cherish her. She was smaller than the village women, not as muscular. Not as hard. The villagers suffered such loss for so many years, hearts hardened. The new baby would be welcome, and coveted.

He lay back, after tucking Solace against him. An arm under his head he gazed at the rock ceiling. A child, his child, their child. Menace was going to be a father. Growing up their village was always on the move, running, and hiding. After his mother died his father grew cold, angry. Menace didn't blame him. The hybrids took more than lives; they took away hope, laughter, love. Everything wonderful, stolen, destroyed, murdered.

There would be no turning back on the new course of action. Their destiny was to win. Menace smiled. If they had a girl he wanted to name her Destiny, a boy

Win. For a second he thought of shaking Solace awake then sighed, she was too tired. He would leave her be for now. It was time to envision his small daughter in his arms, helpless, beautiful, and greatly loved. Or his young son swinging his first sword with Menace, as proud as he could be, watching, helping. He almost laughed aloud when the image in his mind changed to that of his proud daughter swinging the sword. Either sex would be well versed in arms and weapon training.

Rain was pelting against the partitions. Darkness settled into the grumbled rants of one furious with life. Nature hadn't given up its assault on the earth. For now their homes would stay left empty. Menace curled around Solace to keep her warm. He closed his eyes and fell asleep yearning to hold the baby that was inside his beloved.

****

"Solace."

Solace jolted awake to see the concerned face of Kiki staring at her.

"What's wrong?" Solace asked.

"It's Muffin. I think she's having her cubs. The other bulwarks are nervous. The males are growling, Bubble-gum is beside himself. These aren't the alphas pups. What'll we do?"

"Boil some water."

Kiki looked stumped. "Do people really do that?"

"Yes. I want some tea."

Solace smiled at Menace who lay with his eyes open. She leaned down to kiss his cheek then climbed from the furs. Her tummy was queasy. Her legs were stiff from the fast walk back and little sleep. She thanked Aba for a cup of steaming tea and went to join

Clarity at Muffin's side. The bulwark was definitely in labor.

"How soon, do you think?" Solace asked.

"I think right now," Clarity replied.

There was a large hollow in the cave chosen for the birth. The other bulwarks would have to get through many people in order to get to Muffin. The female was snarling, but her wrath was toward the male bulwarks who would kill her offspring, she seemed to understand the humans helping her presented no danger.

The first of her litter was a tiny Bubble-gum miniature. A male. The two larger bulwarks came forward in a threatening manner and to everyone's surprise Bubble-gum went ballistic. He attacked the alpha. The alpha was unprepared and yelped when an ear was torn and a leg bit, drawing blood. Bubble-gum didn't back down when the alpha took a swipe at him. The dog bit the swung claw and held on shaking his head back and forth so hard the bulwark looked like it was dancing.

"Whoa kick ass," Luke said and grinned.

The beta backed off when the alpha retreated once the dog let go. Luke was laughing. Rex slapped a small hand to his forehead. The other female bulwark approached with deference when all three cubs were checked over by their protective mother. The female sniffed the babies from a distance and settled near Muffin. It became apparent quickly it would take a village to raise these cubs. Whether the males liked it or not no one and nothing was going to harm the new additions.

Solace held a tiny female bulwark in her arms. The cub pup was dark with a small patch of white under her chin. She gave a glance to Muffin.

"So you get these tiny little things that come out your big ass body and my baby will be twice as big."

"You are going to have a baby?" Aba was shrieking, laughing, crying. "I haven't seen a baby since I was a baby."

"Yes," Solace said and smiled. "Menace and I are going to have a baby."

"*We're* pregnant," Aba bellowed with glee. "We must know everything. Is that why you're so tired. I want to experience what you are." Many women were nodding in excitement.

"Great." It was Edge's turn to slap a hand to his forehead.

The cave was in an uproar. Solace settled back beside Muffin watching. There was general happiness, some women were in tears. Some men were worried about protecting the new addition. The bulwarks were fine with the children but had never once been exposed to a tiny infant.

"A cave is no place to raise these children let alone a baby, *she* will become chilled," Aba moaned.

"We need to get back to our homes so *he* won't have to worry about hybrids," Edge said.

"*She'll* be fine. It'll be a while before *she's* born," Heath countered.

"*He* has the protection of many," Lochlan pointed out.

Solace made a face and turned to gaze at Clarity. "When did I have fraternal twins?"

"I have no clue."

The bantering continued, with Doom included, about the sex of the baby and where it would be safest.

Solace gave the mini bulwark back to her mother and stood. Everyone stopped arguing and watched her. When she took a step Edge moved a little closer with Aba. Clarity howled with laughter. Solace made her way into Menace's arms, and only then was there a collective sigh of relief she was uninjured by her short walk.

Solace groaned. "This is going to be the longest nine months of my entire life."

"Nine more?" Menace said and gaped.

"I think maybe six or a little less now. Humans normally carry for thirty eight to forty weeks. The time here is difficult to gauge. One day has rolled into another. Soon enough you'll be rolling me around."

Menace chuckled but settled her onto the furs. "It's time for you to eat and rest."

"Good Lord not you too," she whined.

"You may as well take advantage of the moment. There is meat to dry and work around the cave the others will be doing."

"So I have a get out of jail baby pass?"

She could see he was mystified. Menace rose and Solace sat back while everyone made a point to bring her something. She shrugged as all gazes were directed to her midriff as though she should be showing, something. It was a good thing the baby couldn't stick a hand out and wave, they'd all expire.

"I have just become public property." She sighed and settled down to snuggle into the furs. As the rain picked up another fur was placed over her. Solace glanced up expecting Menace but the little T-rex leaned over to lick her cheek, then moved off. "Definitely public property."

****

Menace had Solace by the hand. They were followed by a male bulwark. The males were kept as busy as was possible in their crowded home. Menace wanted quiet time with Solace who complained she was watched every single second. It was true. If she so much as belched her admirers rushed over with water, cold compresses, warm compresses, advice, food.

"Wish we could go home," Solace said.

"Soon, sweetness. The area around our home is almost dry and the grass has begun to grow."

"I want our bed and privacy back."

It was rare for her to pout but when he asked Clarity about Solace's mood changes she laughed and suggested he get used to it. He reminded himself Solace warned him. She was taken over at times by the petulance of her actual *inner* child. Earlier Solace began sobbing while sitting on her furs and watching others work. Rex was horrified and sat and wailed with her. *That was disturbing.* Muffin howled, the children cried, the other females followed along until Doom suggested Menace take Solace for a walk within the caves. When the women said they wanted to experience everything Solace did, they meant it.

Menace carried a thick fur and a pack on his back filled with different foods. Solace would rave over a meal one moment then sit back and claim she couldn't bear to eat another bite. The worst were cravings he had no idea what the strange items were she spoke of. Fries smothered in gravy doused with coleslaw. With Clarity's help they made something similar that resembled barf. For the life of him he would never understand hot dogs, *who eats dogs?* She wanted to dip the dog in ice cream. Ice cream was apparently very cold and somewhat solidified, and runny if warmed. It sounded horrifying. Every time Bubble-gum came close Menace wanted to spirit the poor mutt away.

"Here, see," Menace said. His torch lit a small cubby. He spread the thick warm fur and led Solace to sit. He started a small fire after settling another fur across Solace's shoulders and began to pull packages from his hide pack. Aba sent enough food for ten people. The large roast of mammoth mastodon, Solace said they should rename the creature a mammadon, made her gag so he tossed it to the bulwark. The beast settled in their vision to keep watch.

"Are you warm enough, my love?" he asked.

"Fine."

Solace took a piece of buttered bannock and tucked a small amount of deer meat and a little cheese inside. She took tiny bites. Menace noted she consumed a great deal of water. She was quiet or brooding. Menace reached to tuck a lock of hair from her face, it fell back as though she tried to hide.

"Are you tired from the walk here?" he asked.

"It feels good to stretch my legs and be away from all the prying eyes and commotion. I miss our quiet time together."

"We will have time to ourselves after the baby comes."

She chuckled. "We will have less time. A baby is incredibly demanding."

"Do you really think Aba will hand the baby over once she gets her hands on it? You may have to take up another hobby. Like stalking our own child."

"I will enjoy the peace I know the others will bring.

I've never known a baby wanted more than ours. I keep having weird dreams of a mini T-rex being a nursemaid and wearing an apron. It's beyond disturbing."

Menace agreed and stroked the same lock of hair from her face, it stayed in place this time. She was radiant. "What is it like to carry life? Do you feel different?"

"It's a little odd and wonderful. Something is inside me, our baby, but it has to grow all the time. I wonder how the Neandersauri can stand another person inside them. I wonder if the inner being ever gets angry it can never come out. This baby will be a complete person when it's born. A different individual. He or she is safely inside not growing to adapt to my body, but growing its own. When the Neandersauri move the being inside moves. What if the body within is tired and doesn't want to move? What if the being inside is hungry or thirsty? Does one rule and the other simply follow?"

"I can tell you have been thinking a lot of our enemy."

"I suppose I have been. I wonder if the inner being of the hybrid gets ill. I am sick in the mornings but it's not too bad and some days non-existent. I know the baby is fine and not ill. I also know the baby takes whatever it needs whenever it needs it. I wonder if it works the same for the hybrid."

"I don't know." She appeared agitated and he knew there was more to what she was saying. "What's really bothering you?"

"I'm bored senseless," she wailed. "I spend too much time thinking and less time doing things. I'm going to have to put my foot down. I need to be busy, the tedium is killing me. If I sneeze every other woman repeats the gesture. Everyone wants to rub my tummy or talk to it. Rex is a mother hen. He stares at me and it's creepy. He sees me staring and looks away as fast as he can, then slowly he turns his head and his eyes settle back onto my belly."

The way she explained and her tone made goosebumps rise on his arms. "They are concerned for you."

"I know but there are times I'd like to scream *love me less*."

Menace gathered her into his arms to cuddle. Being the first pregnant female the villagers have ever seen was a novelty, but he could tell the attention was getting to her. Having your every move watched would grate on him so he could only imagine what Solace was feeling. She clung to him and pressed her face into his throat. Her heated breath was welcome. She was warm and soft. His hands stroked her back. Her lips were welcoming when he kissed her. His cock jumped and Menace suppressed a moan of desire. She grew more radiant every day. Having her beside him was torture in a sweet way. Breaking their kiss and leaning over he pressed his forehead to hers.

"Are you going to make love to me or not?"

Menace was surprised by her demanding tone. "My love the baby in there is getting bigger. I can see your belly has rounded out."

"So what?"

"I don't want to hurt our child."

"Menace if you expect me to wait around until this baby comes before having sex you're insane. Lying beside you at night needing you to touch me is torture.

My body screams so loud for you I'm surprised I don't keep the entire cave awake at night. You won't hurt either of us."

"You're certain?"

"Yes," she exploded. "We're finally alone out here. I was so worried if we made love in the cave you'd be attacked by a T-rex trying to protect me. I need, my body wants, so much more than to kiss and cuddle."

His relief flooded his veins. At night he gazed at her beauty needing to do more than hold her. When his throbbing cock engorged his hand would rub her tummy in a tender fashion and he would remind himself his child was tucked safely away. Now she was telling him she wanted him. When there was no bump he wasn't as concerned.

Menace lay her back to untie the sash holding her soft leather hide shirt closed. The fur at her shoulders slipped off. Her breasts spilled free. The nipples puckered in the cooler air. He dipped his head to suckle. A bud was laved to tighten further. Soon these precious gifts would belong to another; but not as yet. More of her firm sweet skin was sucked into his mouth. Her back arched. Menace savored her, enjoying the soft hands she ran across his back and arms.

Small quick kisses came next from breast to belly. Menace rubbed his nose in her navel and smiled.

"Sleep little one. Your father and mother will take good care of you. I will be honored the first time I meet you."

When he gazed at Solace happiness overflowed his being. She gazed back with love. His fingers tugged the clothing at her hips, sliding the hide pants down over her thighs. He tossed her footwear aside. When he reached for her ankle he took a foot into his hands and kissed her instep. Each toe was sucked then released, he saw her shiver and grew concerned.

"Are you cold?" he asked.

"I'm on fire."

Licking his way back up the inside of her leg he paused when he reached her mound. Her soft tuft of female hair was no barrier and his fingers delved deep. Her warm welcome of wet heat made him realize she was ready. He lowered to carefully cover her. Face to face their bodies touched only lightly. When he tasted her he suckled her top lip, then bottom. Their mouths crashed together. Ever so gentle he rose higher and found her opening with his cock.

He rubbed against her letting some spilled eager seed wet her further. She spread her legs, widening her thighs, coaxing him deeper. Inch by inch he thrust.

"Menace, you're killing me."

He stopped moving. "Are you hurt?"

"No, will you get in there already?"

"You have grown demanding the last little while."

"Hello, pregnant lady prone to mood swings."

Menace pushed harder. He heard her sigh. They rocked together enjoying the heat of their bodies, their pleasure at give and take. He thought for a moment to roll her onto him but wanted her beneath him where she was safest.

"I love you, Menace."

"The word love is so small yet means so much," he said and groaned with the effort to be as gentle as possible.

Her insides squeezed and released. Their breath quickened and he lowered his head to kiss her cheek.

Theirs wasn't a harried joining, they loved. Her flesh was warm and soft and he smiled when his belly touched hers. He was building when he felt her wetness and heard her moan. The relief of his climax came soon after. Solace cried out and stilled. Menace slipped to her side and tucked part of the fur over her ass.

"Solace there must be another word for love. What I feel for you is intense, blinding, protective, desire. The words are useless when there is more. Passion, worry, I am engulfed in needing to pick you up and shield you from everything, everyone. The idea expands my chest, my arms grow stronger, yet gentle. My hands, they must touch you. Through them we join with a caress. Your lips drive me crazy, wanting them on mine every single second of the day. Am I insane?"

She chuckled and cupped his cheek. "That's why we have the word love."

"You understand I feel all those emotions with a single word?"

"Yes."

"How?"

"Because I feel the same."

His throat was suddenly burning. "Solace you could never hope to lift me, I'm too heavy."

She laughed. "I do adore you, my love. Since you are already in my heart I have strength."

He contemplated her words. "All right, but how about you refrain from trying to pick me up?"

Solace howled with laughter. The bulwark jumped to its feet and approached. She was chuckling and shoving the beast away from her now bare ass, the fur fell to the side.

"Get away, you big dumb beast. I'm fine," she said

and smiled while patting the furred beast's ruff.

"I think it's time to return to the others," Menace said and pulled on his clothes.

Solace shoved at the beast again while struggling into her pants. "Yes, there's a baby in there. Now get." She stopped for a second. Her gaze grew concerned. "These bulwarks haven't been exposed to babies. Will they try for mine?"

"The beasts will do the bidding of their masters," Menace said. He helped her to rise. "The twins are the youngest yet to ever appear on this planet. You've seen how the beasts interact with them. Muffin's cubs will adore this baby."

"Doom will let the bulwarks all live won't he? Clarity said it's your way to kill the mothers after birth and house the cubs inside with family."

"Clarity would smack him upside the head, I was told if he harmed one. You are right our way was to kill the adults and raise the cubs in our homes, but that's the old way. We will have Muffin raise her own cubs with the villagers in the main area."

"Oh how I want to be home."

"Soon. Soon you will sleep in your own bed. I promise. But the hunters and gatherers will have to go farther afield to find food."

"We'll be all right."

Menace hefted the pack onto his back and the fur into his arms. "Of course we will. I am going to be a father. My son or daughter will be safe and you, my sweetness, will be a wonderful mother. I have my own surprise."

"What would that be?"

"I would ask you let me name our child?"

"You found names didn't you?" She was smiling. "Well?"

"Our daughter should be named Destiny and our son Win."

"I like them both. What do you wish for?"

"I don't need to wish for anything," he said with some confusion. "You are carrying our baby. What is left to wish for?"

"You, my love, are absolutely right."

Chapter Thirteen

The transition from high cave to their village homes was slow. They moved lower down the mountain until each day scouts went out to check the area. At long last, it was determined their domed homes were safe, the ground dry. Food supplies were low and once the villagers settled a hunting party was established. Solace insisted she was well enough to accompany the hunters, while the youngest children stayed behind under the watchful eyes of Aba, a few other village women, and Muffin. The mothering bulwark lounged while both her cubs and the twins crawled over her.

"We need to make a stop," Clarity said.

The tree where the raptors took shelter was empty. Solace was disappointed, she wondered if the mother's arm healed. Clarity lifted the remains of the crude splint. It was well worn and appeared to have been pulled off recently. They moved on.

The world they once knew was ravished, but there were signs of healing. Above, the sun was bright, high, and warm. Solace tilted her face toward the light and basked in the welcome heat. She noted that morning her pants were a bit tighter than the day before, and she loosened her drawstring to allow more room. She was going to look a sight when her hide pants wouldn't be enough to cover her enlarging rounded belly.

The village home was well protected. Only a human hand could open the doors to the dwelling by pressing a certain stone. Each individual living space was attached underground to the main living area. Sixteen homes in all, with the main eating room large and always filled with activity. Outside wasn't safe, at all. Hybrid carnivorous dinosaurs lived on this planet where only the strong survived, and many were moving back to their old stomping grounds.

The monstrosities of the sacrifices took their toll on the people. This was the first year of no slaughter, and human men and women walked with the villagers. Lochlan and Heath came from two different Earths. Only Solace and Clarity were from Lochlan's planet as were the twins, Luke, Nick, Em, Nina and Kiki.

The quiet group was wary of every sound, each bush movement. A clear sky could become a tempest in mere moments. All of the men went bare-chested except Lochlan and Heath who wore vests. Each male decided on buckskin pants or cut-off's at the knee. The women were dressed much the same. All sported what Clarity maintained were booties that formed to the feet. Solace had been annoyed when her boots had to be replaced. Doom insisted once leaving the mountain she would draw too much attention to herself now that the other dinosaurs returned. The material from the megaceros was too different, and intriguing.

They all stopped at a loud booming sound. Creeping over a high-rise they dropped belly down to shimmy to the edge to gaze over. Solace was astounded. Massive creatures were nosing foliage.

"What are those?" Heath asked.

"I've never seen anything like it. That waterway

wasn't there before," Doom said.

"Those are whales," Clarity said.

"But whales live in the ocean," Solace said.

"At one time they lived on land and took to the ocean as humans lived in water and took to land."

The creatures were large with four legs. Long snouts protruded. "But where are real whales?" Solace asked.

Clarity grinned at her. "They're different to be certain." She then sobered. "I was afraid of this. If continents separated we may see animals we've never seen before. Animals that once stayed away may have been forced closer. Anything could be out there. Megalodon's, super-squids or even dunkleosteus."

"A who watsis?" Luke asked.

Clarity chuckled. "It was said to be a thirty-foot tank with teeth. This planet has turned to super hybrids. So who knows if there's a pure basilosaurus or sea scorpions."

"Look." Doom pointed. "The isolated one. We'll go around and get that one."

"Aw," Solace said. "Not a whale."

"We need fresh food," Menace said.

"We may also have another source of food," Clarity said.

"If the ocean is close we can gather seaweed," Solace said with excitement. "You have seafood, I ate it last year. If the ocean has moved we can find more fish and pickle it, or salt it."

"We have in the past salted large fish for the long sleep," Doom said. "The sea wasn't as close and it was a long walk but worth the effort."

"You may have to include more than fish from the

sea. You need to adapt to survive. I'm thinking lobster and crab would be tasty right now. Or shrimp, what I wouldn't give for a fresh sardine sandwich. Those oysters you dried and brought back tasted so good," Solace said.

"Can we hunt, please?" Lochlan said. "All this food talk is making me hungry. I heard a growl and thought it was a saber—it was my guts."

"It's a whale, how do you eat whale?" Heath said. His sad tone made Lochlan scowl.

"With salt and pepper. It's food, you ninny, food. Why not send a few to make a camp and we can hunt?" Lochlan suggested.

Some stayed behind, including Heath who Solace thought might be stinging from Lochlan's reproach, and made a small camp while the others went to hunt. The hunters dispatched the whale creature. Gutting the being was hard work and everyone helped. At camp, food was roasted while they worked. They ate a quick meal with some tea and lugging large packs and pulling numerous travois they headed for the village. The group stayed close allowing none to trail behind.

They dropped their supplies when they came across five Neandersauri roaming the village. Doom and the other men engaged in battle. Five young hybrids were no match for the skilled warriors. The Neandersauri were killed and dragged far away into the bush then dropped off a high cliff into a waterfall.

Solace made her way to the bed in her room; she was tired from the long day. She sat on the raised platform of high furs. Everything inside remained airtight and dry. Wearily she dropped her footwear to the ground, her pants next, then unlaced the rawhide string at her vest, her breasts spilling free. She groaned as she lay back.

"Oh my boobs ache." Menace sat beside her. He lifted his hand. "Touch my tit and die," she said with a growl.

He pulled back his hand. "I only wanted to massage them."

His gaze was innocent enough but she saw the sparkle behind his eyes. "Massage this." She rolled to wiggle her ass.

Huge fingers settled onto firm flesh, digging and dragging his way over her rounded rump. He worked his way over her thighs and to her calves. Each foot was picked up and the pads of his thumbs took away the tension. Back up he went over her body to her back. Her shoulders were screaming *oh God yes* as he continued.

Solace had balled a fur up under her arms and turned slightly to keep weight from her belly and boobs. He nudged her onto her back. A tentative touch to a breast and she groaned. Menace was careful. He began at the base and with only a thumb rubbed in small circles easing a full sensation. Both high mounds were given attention. As were her arms, hands and fingers.

Her throat was rubbed to her shoulders and he made his way to her rounded belly. He leaned down for a kiss at her navel. Solace remembered those hands dispatching two hybrid Neandersauri in a fury. How dare those creatures be near their home? How far had these proud villagers come, before hiding and afraid to become ferocious and daring. Menace always had the spark of defiance, and when given the means to react and defend others a fiercely deadly side was born.

"Sleep little one, your father is here to care for you."

"Why don't you come to bed to sleep?" Solace said.

"There is much to be done with the whale creature. Clarity says the blubber is useful. I thought it was a female who blubbered when she cried."

Solace laughed. "Women don't blubber when we cry, we express emotion."

"I'll remember that the next time you sob your heart out when a tie breaks on your booties. Grown men avoid you when you lose your temper."

She smacked his chest. "Remember those emotions aren't all mine. I'm hormonal not homicidal."

"Tell that to the bug you ran through with your sword."

"Hey in my defense those things are huge. The mere fact I did kill it with a sword is proof. And those grown men run because when I lose my temper, you get a glare to your eye that says; *touch my female and die*."

He sighed and slid in beside her. "I suppose it's true. I'm a little overprotective."

"A little?" she sputtered.

"Now I have a larger problem. I was worried about bringing you along for the hunt, then we return to find hybrids roaming our village in daylight. I am needed to hunt but you and our baby need me more."

Solace cuddled into his arms. "The hybrids can't break in."

"What if they can?"

She stiffened. "What do you mean?"

"I studied a young hybrid as I pulled him away. Before throwing him into the falls I became curious.

Why would they venture so close? What was there to gain when they knew nothing could penetrate our locks. The rocks only slide back when touched by a human or villager. I sliced its outer hand off. Solace, the hand within was smaller, almost human. What if there is a single hybrid with a human hand within?"

She sat up. Menace rubbed her hip but lay flat. "Would they cut off their own hand to seek entry?"

"If they can gain entry by any means what do you think?"

"They would in a heartbeat. We have to tell Doom."

"I did. Clarity asked me to remember what the hand looked like. It was soft and flat." He took Solace's fingertip into his hands and traced her prints. "There were none of these spirals such as the villagers have and humans have."

"Each person's is unique. No one has the same set of prints except maybe twins. Identical twins. Blue and Cole are fraternal. If they discover the difference, if there is a difference, we will be in for trouble. What's to stop them from hunting a human and cutting off a hand to hold to a door? Would they be that smart?"

"They want space flight but the human hand must be warm. That means they would need to cut a hand from a person right near the door. The hybrids would continue to try if they thought it might work," Menace said.

"All the villagers in all areas need to be warned. The Neandersauri must all be killed."

"They will be here…"

"That's right. Clarity said she thinks the continents split and those whales must be proof. The ocean is closer to us. If a hybrid wants space flight they sure as hell will be able to build a decent boat," Solace said.

"But not today," Menace said. "It was a long walk and you're tired. Rest. When you wake it will be time to eat in the main hall. Sleep, my love. I'll keep you safe. There are others watching. The bulwarks are outside. Muffin is in the main hall with her cubs. She has heightened senses these days."

"My sense of smell has increased. I guess I notice more when something has an odor to it."

Solace settled beside him, his unique scent was a magnet. Worry made sleep elusive but eventually the rigors of the day caught up to her. She closed her eyes and drifted into worried dreams.

****

Menace jolted awake. Solace was slumbering by his side. He'd fallen asleep when he meant only to rest. What woke him? From the recess of his mind he remembered a baby cry. Menace was very young, perhaps five at the time, or no more than the age of the twins. There was soft weeping. An anguished cry that was silenced. The baby's mewling wail was cut short. The hybrids that were following his father's village came into view. A hand went over Menace's mouth, he remained quiet knowing quiet was safety. The hybrids passed by.

An icy finger slid down Menace's spine. The baby was never seen. Killed after birth. Sparing the child a life of running and saving the villagers from detection. If the parents were killed there would be no one left to care for the babe. Or if not able to quiet the child immediately, an entire village could perish. The mother had no choice. Sacrifice one for many.

All children brought to any village learned fast to keep silent when warned. A baby could not. Fear built inside. If the hybrids could gain entry there would be no hiding for Solace if the baby were born. He bolted upright. A new room had to be made before the baby's birth. Soundproof, impenetrable, more so than the homes already were. Well stocked with provisions. Something more impassable than the room used for hibernating. The room would be in need of something more. His mind was racing with his heart, the babe's cries in his dreams resounded in his ears, worse was the sudden silence. Only one print would be able to activate the door lock to this new oasis. *Whose?* No not who, what.

Bubble-gum was the only dog on the planet. A failsafe. Menace woke Solace and they made their way to the main hall. When they sat he revealed his plan. Doom looked skeptical. Clarity was confident he was on to something. The dog was loyal, motivated by food and praise. Highly trainable. The first thing they had to do was build a new room.

"Over here in an out of the way place." Menace was pacing off against a wall.

He took long strides indicating how long the room should be. Breaking through the hard wall was impossible from top side. A massive hole would have to be dug first. Inside, it was easier to break through the solid rock, especially when Clarity devised a sledgehammer. They began immediately. Once they broke free to the dirt, the going was easier.

Huge hides of dirt were hauled away and used in what was to be a garden Clarity wanted to grow. Before their food was accessible and close to home. Plant life was all but wiped out nearby. When the gatherers went out they brought back plants with roots attached and began cultivating their new garden above ground. The idea of the mouflon nagged the corner of Menace's mind. There were no such small manageable creatures on his planet, unless the storms scattered a creature of the same type closer. He then remembered seeing the trail of a goat-like creature on the mountain. They were elusive and huge. If caught, they would need to be penned inside like they were at the treehouse. The little goat-like creatures intrigued Menace and he noted not all the animals were the same. He gazed at the hybrid cubs, the female was going to be a bit larger than her father but no more. If the villagers could capture the smallest of the mouflon hybrids they could cultivate the size they wanted over time.

As the rebuilding and new building of their lives unfolded, each person was necessary for survival. Other villagers visited, no longer separated from others by the Neandersauri. One other village was expecting a human child to be born and those visiting were relieved to find a plan of action could be initiated. The only problem was Bubble-gum was unique. So too were his offspring. The visiting village lost its last bulwark to old age.

Muffin's cubs were too young as yet to be taken from their mother but in a couple of months the village could return and adopt one of the males. Clarity wanted the only female. She planned on breeding more of the massive creatures. With any luck after the cubs were weaned Muffin and Bubble-gum might be tempted to procreate.

The small bundles of fur were a favorite. They played with the children inside and out. Already grown to the twins' height they were gentle while tussling but their mother was teaching them to be watchful. The cubs would prove to be invaluable with their parents' gentleness, intelligence, and protective nature.

"Do we gotta give a baby away?" Blue asked Menace.

"The other village needs a bulwark for safety. We have many," Menace said.

"Are you going to give us away now that you're having your own baby?" the boy was solemn when he asked.

"I can't give away a child who is like my own," Menace said. "You're stuck with me."

Blue smiled and wrapped his arms around Menace's neck.

****

Time for the villagers flew by. There was much to do. Hunting for hibernation was paramount. The new safe room was finished. Solace grew larger and Menace found he wanted to keep his hands on her belly. So did many others. She was good natured, but there were times he could see her lips pressed together and Menace did his best to take away from the hustle of so many often.

Today was one of those days Solace needed to be free of the numerous questions of how *exactly* was she feeling. Once weaned, Muffin and one young but large male walked to the village expecting the new baby with Menace, Doom and others. Solace insisted seeing where the cub would live so Muffin would be able to visit. They entered the villagers' home area. Immediately the bulwarks were wary.

There were no villagers to greet them. Inside told

of the disaster. The Neandersauri finally found a way to enter what was deemed impenetrable. The male villagers were dead, their heads split. The females gone.

"If we don't find those females fast and the hybrids have more of their own females those women won't last long," Solace said.

She was petrified and Menace was furious with himself for bringing her. Farther along in her pregnancy she was still able to move comfortably but the distention in her belly was clearly noticeable. He wanted to run to her and lift her into his arms. Instead he wrapped an arm around her shoulder. Her concern was for the others.

"Muffin, find them. Find the humans," Clarity demanded of the beast. A trick Clarity had been working on. If the children were ever forced into hiding the adults wanted to be able to find them once the danger passed.

Both Muffin and her offspring set to work. Soon all were following a path. One by one the females were found dead. Their bellies left alone the hybrids wanted only DNA and stem cells from brains.

"Does this mean there are no more hybrid females?" Clarity wondered aloud.

"Maybe the female's screams were too much. The face of this one has claw marks where a hybrid tried to silence her. She was killed by accident. The hybrids hunting are yearlings. Another pack must have formed," Menace said scanning the area.

"Where's the expectant mother?" Solace asked.

A scream from the foliage had them all running. Muffin was the first to attack. Swords were drawn. The pregnant female was alive but unconscious. Muffin and her baby stood over her, growling, making lunges with sharp claws. Swords were slicing at talons. An arrow pierced a hybrid under its nose and Menace turned to see Nick. The boy came and went as he pleased. Comfortable with the planet and surroundings. Kiki had been teaching him to use new weapons. A sword his size and lightweight, hung at his belt on his hip. For now the teen and Doom gave one another a wide berth. Before his anger for Doom came the hybrids, a being Nick loathed with his heart and soul. With skill Nick managed to fell three from his high advantage point.

Nick was the only young earth human with the group and they didn't know he'd been following. The children said a tearful goodbye to Muffin's baby before the group set out earlier. The cub was never given a name; he was supposed to be given away. That was no longer the case. One by one the hybrids fell until they fled. Doom picked up the pregnant female, who appeared to be as far along as Solace. They carried her back to their village, a lone survivor.

When the woman woke she sobbed uncontrollably and explained they were sitting down to lunch when the attack occurred. They were stormed by a pack of fifteen. Without an adult to supervise the young hybrids were running wild in packs. They wanted to start their own breeding but there were no females. It became apparent the village females would fight and many did to the death. Until she, Amy, was alone.

The hybrids used clicks and whistles to speak but there were few words as well. Amy realized they were taking her to keep until her baby was born. If there were no Neandersauri hybrids left they would cultivate their own humans. Starting with her. They planned to capture humans and breed them.

"Astute, really," Clarity said.

"Scary as shit," Solace said.

"I think your idea to mass produce bulwarks is a good one," Doom said to Clarity.

"Since they're weaned and grow at a fast rate we should have a number of them by next spring," Solace said.

Doom jumped on a table in the main hall. "We killed at least ten hybrids. Three thanks to Nick." Menace saw Nick's head snap up at the praise. The normal scowl softened for a brief second especially when Kiki and Nina hugged him. "We can't allow what happened to those at the other village happen to us. We need to hunt for hybrids as much as for food."

"That's going to be hard," Menace said. "Why not two hunting parties? One for hybrids and another for food and plants? Before, the hybrids left us alone when we hunted, because we were keeping their sacrifices safe. They wanted us alive so the decrease in sacrifices wouldn't happen. Not anymore. It's every villager and hybrid for himself."

"What about home?" Aba said wringing her hands. "The safe shelter is ready, but we need to add dried foods. Everyone must help to find all that we'll need for the great sleep. When we waken, we must gorge or die. That means leaving many women behind to care for the children. Packs of desperate hybrids will do anything. Before, they didn't go after our young, which may change."

"You're right about that. These young hybrids have no direction," Doom said.

"I've been working with Bubble-gum and his

cubs." Menace reached to pet the dog's head. We need to change the locks on all outside doors today. No one gets in without a cub or Bubble-gum. Every damned hybrid can cut off its mangy hand for the one inside but they will never get in."

"We've been reduced to being let in by a dog. What's that the kids sing? Who let the dogs out? Well now it'll be who let the human's in," Edge grumbled.

Luke howled with laughter, which made Rex chuckle.

"Starting today," Doom said and cocked his head. "We will sleep with no fear."

"Easy for you to say," Solace grumbled. "You never gave birth. Try popping a watermelon out a vagina."

"Look out," Luke yelled. "She has that look. Run and hide. Duck for cover."

All of the kids screamed in mock horror and raced under the tables. Including the cubs and Bubble-gum. Edge gave a wry smile to Menace.

"Well I'll sleep tonight. Solace is scary when pissed."

Solace snapped her teeth at him.

Chapter Fourteen

"How are you feeling?" Clarity asked Solace.

"Better since starting my third trimester. I'm not fat, yet. I think my mood swings are under control, for the most part. A certain smell doesn't send me running for a basket to puke. Why these people insist on having outdoor plumbing is beyond me."

"Doom is hilarious when I mention an indoor toilet. He gets all offended about shitting inside the home. I remind him we have night baskets."

"Menace is the same way. Although I think he likes having to come with me when I go out to the caves. That wasn't so in the beginning when I had to pee every five minutes. I'm glad that's over, at least for now. I'm worried about being outside with my pants down when I'm too fat to see my feet."

"Did you talk to Menace about what we spoke of?" Clarity asked.

"I know I should. I wonder what the village women did during pregnancy if any gave birth during hibernation. Or what I'll do if Menace is hibernating when I give birth. Amy mentioned she's afraid of the same thing."

"I did sort of mention it to Doom, about their females, not you. He said their females never gave birth during that time. Shortly after, but not one case did he remember where a woman emerged from the big sleep with a baby, mind you he was the last born he reminded me. As for Amy I noted Heath and Lochlan fussing over her. Neither of them have to hibernate."

Solace and Clarity were trailing behind a search party. Menace and Doom were in the lead with Muffin followed by Lochlan, Edge, Nick, Kiki, and Luke. Rex had been left home much to his annoyance. Bongo trailed Solace and Clarity. Nick was a necessity. He was adept at finding caves and places the hybrids might be hiding. The teen seldom smiled and maintained his hatred of Doom but was quick to see the advantage of living in a large group.

"Here." Nick was pointing.

The others ventured forward. Inside a large cavern was filled with baskets of roots and other edible vegetation. A storage area for when hibernation set in. Solace knew it wouldn't be touched, for now by either human or hybrid. When the heavy snow hit earth, humans would be back to poison the food. During the big sleep the hybrids slumbered as well for weeks until rising once to gorge. They would return to their hide out and sleep again until the worst of winter and heavy snows passed.

"I wonder if they've started storing meat," Menace said.

The cavern was only in the midst of being stocked. If the food was close it meant the hybrids were. They ventured from the cave to return home.

"Doom," Solace said. "Instead of poisoning the food why don't we send our people in to kill the hybrids before they wake and take their food?"

"I thought of that," he replied. "What if these are decoys and already poisoned?"

"With food so scarce do you think they'd try it?" Clarity asked.

"Yes. We are. Plus they're young and second guessing more than we are. Instead of taking the food and leaving them to starve it's safer to poison the food. They may think we're stupid or too afraid. They're cocky little bastards," Menace said.

"Menace is right," Doom said. "I know it looks like we don't have much but tomorrow we're headed to where the milk creatures give birth. The hybrids will be there in force wanting to kill and eat the creatures and store them. We won't attack the creatures but if the hybrids have killed we will take the meat for ourselves."

"We'll have to be diligent then. Those who stay behind will be in as much danger." Menace gazed at Solace. "I want you in the safe room with the youngsters."

"But..."

"It's all right Solace," Clarity interrupted. "I'm staying behind too. At the first sign of trouble we can all wait it out until the hunters return. We can pack up a few essentials to tide us over if we need to hide."

Solace gave her a fast glance. Clarity had a tendency to do things when Doom wasn't underfoot unless there was another reason, Clarity seemed tired as of late. Her friend said nothing to indicate if she was sick. Their trek back to the homes wasn't in vain. They scared up a flock of small chicken-like dinosaurs and killed eight. Other gatherers had been fortunate as well. After dinner Menace and Solace retired for the evening.

"How do you feel?" Menace asked.

"Fine. A bit worried about tomorrow."

"The hybrids can't get in. Muffin and her cubs are staying behind with the other female bulwark and Bubble-gum. Bulwarks are loyal beings and the hybrids have no use for them. Rex will come with us and Bongo. You'll be safe. I don't think it's occurred to the hybrid youngsters to band together. They live in groups but in each group there is one leader. All the leaders are dead and no one has direction. I'm guessing there is huge dissention amongst them."

"I suppose."

Menace kissed her. Solace melted against him. Chest to chest they roamed their hands over one another pulling at clothing until they lay naked. She wanted him fast and he sensed her need. Solace lay back and Menace plunged into her heat. Swift movement had her breath catch. He was powerful when filled with passion.

She lifted her legs to wrap around his waist and when she came her body trembled. Solace shivered when he roared. Menace collapsed beside her. Solace cuddled next to him. It was a long time before either fell asleep.

****

When morning came the hunters gathered in the main room and checked weapons. Heath and a few others stayed behind. Solace knew Menace was torn between staying and going. She promised him she would be safe. After they left, Clarity gathered everyone around. They were soon doing various tasks previously overlooked. The children made new matches, while others began the tedious process of making paper for balloons.

Bombs were assembled. Clarity and Solace wanted to make certain if when they were outside everyone would have access to easy weapons. Solace heard giggling and watched the twins crawl over Muffin. Headfirst Blue slid landing on outstretched hands, his twin laughing. The child was up and waved his hands in the air.

"I'm starving to death," Blue whined. The female cub had attached her teeth to the seat of his pants and was pulling.

"Me too," Cole concurred, he grabbed the cub by her short tail, trying to aid his brother.

The smaller of the two male cubs grabbed Cole's hide pants and pulled. Em knew better than to pull a tail but wrapped her arms around the male cub's hind legs. Muffin lolled on her side at the commotion.

"Nina will you help me get some lunch ready for this boisterous bunch?" Solace asked.

"Sure." The teen was chuckling.

When the largest male cub began growling everyone stood motionless. Muffin was on her feet. Her teeth bared and her cubs were soon behind her. All passageways from each sixteen rooms were sealed off from the main room. Solace ushered the children into the safe room as quickly as possible, a twin under each arm. As she set the boys on their feet a door slid open. No one moved, or breathed. A female hybrid stood smiling at them. In her arms was a child hybrid cub. It was the most bizarre thing Solace had ever encountered. The smell of the little being must have confused Muffin because she stopped growling to sniff the air.

The hybrid stepped back and male Neandersauri spilled into the room. Solace and Clarity drew swords. Chaos ensued. Heath attacked with a vengeance Solace didn't know he possessed, while Amy fled to the safe room. His sword raised and clashed, Heath smashed repeatedly into hybrids until he went down from a hard blow sending him crashing into tables and chairs. Heath lay still. The female hybrid squealed and whistled orders. The beasts wanted Clarity and Solace. Two cubs tore into the hybrids, felling the beasts in a frenzy, but there were too many. Muffin was fighting three. The hybrids weren't after a fight but trying to keep the others from getting between them and the prizes they sought.

The room Solace pushed the youngsters in was sealed. Aba went down followed by another and another. Blood was flowing in their home. Solace was grabbed into powerful arms. Muffin was enraged and ripped through the three on her to aid Solace. Muffin attacked and ripped the hybrids throat out, Solace slipped to the ground and crawled for a sword. Three more hybrids went after Muffin. Solace was yanked into powerful arms again and the creature began pulling her from the domed home. Bubble-gum grabbed the hybrid by the ankle. The beast smashed the dog over the head and sent him reeling. Last moment Solace saw Clarity yanked into the safe haven by Nina and Em. Em cried out for Solace but Solace screamed at them to close the door.

Solace knew if the hybrids took her away they would leave the others alone. Too many of theirs were down. The arm around her waist was hurting her and she tried to shove it down off her middle.

"You're crushing my baby," she cried out. The hybrid lowered his arm.

The other hybrids followed the one carrying

Solace. She didn't struggle for the baby's safety. The young hybrids weren't gentle with humans; it wasn't bred into them. Any wrong moves and she would be ripped apart. They traveled fast. Her weight was of no concern to the one who had her. The cave in the hill came up quicker than she expected, it was so close to the domed homes. From there she had an eagle's eye view of their village. They were being watched, studied.

Set in a corner on furs Solace waited. A male bulwark beast was tethered, snapping and snarling. Solace gazed at the baby. The child was Neandersauri but covered in fur throughout most of its body. The female holding the baby laughed.

"It takes little time for a hybrid to have offspring. Especially when another beast begins the process. We killed the female for her eggs to mix with mine. Three were born, we kept the lock that works, ugly as it is."

Solace understood her. Her speech was clipped, deep and words were a hiss and whistle, but she was wide-eyed.

"You mated with a bulwark?"

"I'm not a human you imbecile."

No she wasn't. She looked like the other hybrids. Not quite seven feet, rainbow eye color, a fringe of a triceratops was ear-to-ear pulsing with flowing red veins. The baby hybrid had a very small fringe and black eyes.

"You created that little one to open our doors." It was the bulwark in her that must have confused the lock that allowed Bubble-gum and offspring entry. The lock would have detected warmth, fur and perhaps the pads of a hand-paw. They'd outsmarted themselves by thinking the lock was unique when it detected bulwark.

"Of course. This was our key. You humans have nowhere to go that is safe even if you change your locks. We can get to you any time during the day or night, but we do not have to anymore. We have you. The villagers will do what we say, or you will die."

The way the hybrid callously tossed the baby to another made Solace want to vomit. The baby was set on the ground and crawled to the bulwark, who sniffed her then settled. The hybrids began whistling and clicking. No more human words were spoken. Solace studied the hybrid baby. It gazed at her with curiosity. She detected little intelligence. It was cute in an ugly way. It was covered in a dark mat of fine fur. This little thing might be their undoing.

"Do you wish to kill it?"

Solace was startled when the hybrid female came forward. "What?" she asked.

"Go ahead, kill it. It served its purpose. You humans are no doubt changing the lock to your homes as we speak."

"You are animals."

"No *you* are the animals."

"Yet, *you* still don't understand space flight."

"We will. It's only a matter of time. Will your mate exchange the other female for you? Will he kill Doom to save your life? DaV-nin was my father. He would enjoy seeing Doom die, if Doom hadn't killed him."

Her words sent a tingle of fear through Solace. She hoped Menace would come quick. Solace knew he would. Her gaze went to the baby. What of that creature? How was it possible? A flicker of information from an old class at college. Mammal-like reptiles.

What era? *Think.* Permian. Almost all the creatures were wiped out because of a severe draught and loss in oxygen. The Neandersauri were clever. They were even more deadly than she imagined.

****

When the hunters reached the birthing site, a group of ten hybrids were slaughtering the milk-giving creatures. The humans and their animals raced to aid the creatures. Five of the hybrids were slaughtered in a fast furious battle, the rest fled. The sea creatures were wary at first, but after coaxing and soft words understood these were the humans who protected them. The many containers the hunters brought were being filled with precious milk.

"That wasn't as bad as I thought it would be," Doom said.

"Maybe a little too easy," Menace said. He scanned the area clutching his blood-covered sword. The hybrids not only ran, but they left their fallen and their kills behind. "They know we'll take the milk and their kills. These carcasses aren't poisoned. We normally don't hunt these creatures, because we take the milk, but we have eaten them before when slaughtered by other animals."

"The hybrids are young and don't know who to turn to for authority, they keep attacking us or whatever in small roaming gangs," Doom said.

"We were basically handed food and milk. In return for what?" Menace pondered.

"The homes are safe."

"My gut is telling me something is wrong."

"It's dangerous to return alone."

Menace gave him a sidelong glance. "I'll keep that

233

in mind."

There was something inside Menace telling him to go back, fast. He wasted no time. On the move his feet flew over the terrain. A herd of mammoth mastodons gave him a wide berth. A velociraptor hissed as he went by then quieted, two little ones nipped playfully at his heels but Menace didn't have time for them. When Menace reached the domed homes he heard weeping and children crying. Clarity's voice gave him a semblance of release then terror.

"We'll get her back."

Menace flew down the open door wondering why it was open. Clarity jumped up to greet him and Em was soon in his arms sobbing.

"They took Solace," Em said, crying her fear.

"Who?"

"A hybrid offspring bulwark opened the door," Clarity said, tears in her eyes. "There were so many Neandersauri. They killed a few of our villagers and a male bulwark was found dead outside, the beta. Heath and Aba are wounded. Muffin is exhausted. I don't know what happened to the other male bulwark."

"The alpha male followed us," Menace said and swore, goosebumps dotted his arms, his heart was racing in terror for Solace and their babe.

Menace sent a gaze around the room and saw Heath sprawled out, with a pad on his chest soaked in his blood. Aba was lying on a fur near a fire moaning, as were others. Muffin was on her side heaving with Bubble-gum pacing. Tables were overturned, the room was in shambles. The other female bulwark was also groaning and laying on her side.

"Where are the boys and Nina?" Menace asked.

"They are asleep in the safe room with Nina watching them," Clarity said.

A cub sat under a small shelf pressed to the wall. The littlest one, the female. Menace set Em on her feet and took Clarity by her shoulders.

"I'm going after Solace."

"You can't go alone."

"Send Doom and the others when they return."

Menace grabbed more weapons and took off. The biggest of the male cubs trailed him briefly until Menace noticed him. He hunkered down and gazed at the beast. Smaller than his mother but larger than his father the cub was intelligent. This one was definitely going to grow up to be an alpha.

"Well little Alpha cub that's as good a name as any. Go my furry friend, find Solace."

Menace was terrified. If the alien was watching he'd grab Solace and take her away for good. The hybrids couldn't get their hands on more knowledge. Solace knew of battle, she knew their plans and she knew Clarity could give them the means of flight as well as guns and bombs. The young bulwark led him to a cave he knew nothing about. From his position he could see the cave had a clear view of their homes. The Neandersauri were spying on them; all this time. Neandersauri milling around the entrance, seemed to be on high alert. The bulwark raised its gums in a snarl but there was no sound. Man and beast remained out of sight.

The cub skirted the hybrids and took Menace toward the side where a small entrance was. The bulwark was smart for one so young, Muffin had taught him well. The children taught little Alpha and his cub-mates hide and seek. The beast incorporated it into tracking. The pair slipped silently inside.

When Menace saw Solace huddled in a corner rage filled him. Her arms were wrapped around her middle. A small furry creature crawled toward her then shied back, then forward. Menace sucked in his breath when he saw the thing had a child-like face, yet not. Innocence, he was gazing upon pure innocence. He then noted the little creature's hand-paws and suppressed a groan. He understood how the hybrids came to be able to open their lock.

Solace was sitting on a fur rug. There was a tied male bulwark in a corner also watching the small creature-baby. The little thing finally inched toward Solace and touched her hand. She didn't move but smiled to encourage it.

"I won't hurt you," Solace crooned.

Both baby-creature and woman were wide-eyed. A slight sound and Menace shifted. There was a female hybrid watching the exchange, her face a mask of hate. Menace peered closer. There was a familiar resemblance to the female that tugged at Menace's memory. *DaV-nin.* The female was the leader's offspring. The hybrid must have been housed at a different cave. Menace thought they killed all of DaV-nin's young. If there was this female there could be more.

"Go ahead, kill it," the female hybrid said on a snarl.

"No." Quiet dignity rolled off his beloved's tongue.

"Then I will. It is useless and dumb as dirt."

Solace was up, the baby between her legs and Menace knew she meant to protect it. Menace was on the move. He sliced into the female hybrid who shrieked and dropped to her knees. The baby-creature crawled toward the female Neandersauri sobbing and tried to climb on her chest. Others were racing into the cave and Menace tossed Solace a sword. They fought back to back with little Alpha fearlessly snapping and snarling.

Screaming shouts were heard from outside. Other villagers had followed. The fight inside was dragged outside and below the cave. Doom was there and Edge, Lochlan swung his weapon slicing into a hybrid and downing it. The battle raged as limbs fell. Soon the ground was slick with blood. Muffin and her other cubs were in the foray as well as Bongo who protected Kiki. Rex was whacking a downed hybrid on the head with a wooden sword. Menace didn't know why they were all there but was filled with gratitude.

The bright sun sparkled off the red liquid. A breeze blew to ruffle hair, fur and grass. Swords clashed with claws, bombs began to go off. There were more hybrids than they thought and were soon outnumbered. Only Doom's villagers fought this time. Menace pummeled the hybrids with hammering blows keeping Solace close. She tired and her sword drooped, her hand was on her belly. A rumbling of the earth was heard and many were knocked to the ground as the earth split.

The plane, when it came through the dark hole, was large and different. Sleek, black, rounded and equipped with machine guns. Bastian and Tain were firing weapons. Their seats swung in circles in different directions. The hybrids went down. There was some anarchy until Lochlan whooped the cavalry was here. Menace raised his sword in the air and the battle began anew. All of the hybrids must die. There was a means of flight here they mustn't have.

Menace heard Solace scream before he felt the pain slice across his back. He blinked in disbelief. He knew he was dead before he hit the ground. He never got a chance to see his baby.

Chapter Fifteen

Solace screamed and killed the hybrid who downed Menace. Menace lay on his side. She heard Clarity bellow to the wind. Solace dropped beside him, her shaking hands splayed. She couldn't believe what she was seeing.

"No," she cried out, her hands fisted in anguish. *"Nooo."*

The alien appeared surprising her. Solace gazed up at him in shock, her heart pounded in her chest. Solace wanted to stretch out beside her love.

Doom was soon near. "Solace, I'm so sorry. Your friends have helped us kill the hybrids. None are left to lick their wounds."

"This wasn't supposed to happen," Solace whimpered.

"Yes, it was meant to be. It is time for these souls to be released," the alien said and she watched his approach. It was then Solace filled with anger. He knew Menace was to be killed, it was the alien's intention all along.

"You can't take him from me, and you can't take me from here," she said and glared. "Not after everything we've been through. Why let me come home if you were going to let Menace die?"

"Have faith. Watch. They will go home to be reborn."

True to his word the tattoos came to life, images turned to faces and Solace saw them smiling at her. The people were bright yellows, oranges and reds. They walked off into the air. Each person turned to a blazing light. She watched as bodies became a fine sheet turning into an accordion to fold higher as the feet legs and thighs disappeared up into the atmosphere. The small balls of fire gained in intensity, gathering momentum to spread into the heaven.

"They will grow and gather more, and thicker particles will land on another fledgling Earth. A showering of meteors will last for thousands of years with precious DNA enclosed. We have found a new planet," the alien said. "By knocking the meteor against your planet into the other, the wayward planet that would have formed with yours has found its own atmosphere. It's a new beginning."

"What about Menace?" Solace wiped a tear away. Gazing down at his tanned flawless body she noted no blood.

"My gift to him for holding the souls needed is life. Your children will have need of him. Especially the son and daughter you carry within you now."

The alien vanished. Menace groaned and struggled to sit. Solace crushed him to her chest. The plane leveled out and came to a halt. The men disembarked. Amidst the familiars was another. A man from another earth much like the one they were on. Huge, serious, angry. His name was Chaos. From an alternate earth as was theirs.

The hybrids scattered around were dead. The new man approached assessing all. Chaos was as large as Menace, bald, eyes so dark they appeared black. The clothing he wore was much the same as what men on Doom's planet wore but he wasn't covered in tattoos. Except one. A black patch of round ink was on his shoulder with intricate green designs.

"We found this guy on an earth a lot like this one. In fact we thought he was Doom until Joey told us no," Joe said.

"I am Doom. I am happy to have your help, but why are you here?" Doom asked.

"We came for Lochlan," Bastian said. The large man smiled. "We don't leave our own behind."

Lochlan smiled, and the men clasped hands. Rex nipped at Joey's ass and Luke swatted the T-rex with a wooden sword.

"What do we do with this?" Kiki was kneeling on the ground studying the baby-hybrid. The tiny being was huddled in the dirt whimpering.

"It's harmless," Chaos said, dismissing it. "They are on my planet. There is no malice in them. Our hybrids wanted something sinister to battle us, they got fluffy mindless balls of fur."

"It's cute in an ugly way," Kiki said.

"Well who's going to care for it?" Doom demanded.

"We all will." Solace smiled and picked up the hybrid baby. "She can be a playmate to our twins."

"Twins?" Menace asked as he stood.

"It would appear we have a Win and a Destiny quite literally in fact when you gaze at the dead hybrids," Solace said.

"It's time to go back to the village," Doom said.

"What about the plane?" Solace asked.

"We came for Lochlan and anyone else who wants

to go," Joe said. "We need to hurry. That crazy alien said we could take who we wanted but we better move fast. The other planet is a decent place to raise a family." He gazed with meaning at Solace.

"My home is with Menace, here," Solace said.

Joe caught Lochlan's attention. "Well?"

Lochlan's gaze was thoughtful. "Thanks, but I think I'll stick around here for a while."

"Suit yourself," Tain said and clapped him on the back.

Solace hugged Joey. "Take care of your dad."

Joey smiled and hugged her back. "I will. I need to get him on the plane. I didn't realize Edge was so much bigger than my daddy."

Solace chuckled. They loaded the plane and as they flew into the air a sinkhole opened sending those on the ground to their knees. The sleek vessel slipped into the unknown and was gone. Menace pulled Solace into his arms and they moved off.

****

"What's happening on your planet?" Menace asked Chaos.

"Meteors began to hit. The phenomena began before I was born. The rock-like substance brought DNA of different species. New human life is forming but it's strange in a way never seen. This little mutant hybrid is nothing compared to what has come to my planet. So far the new species keep to themselves. Our volcanoes are erupting, ash is forming in the air and it's getting colder. A hypercane formed and there are maybe five percent of my people left. The species forming are adapting. The alien came to me and brought the plane. He said there is one last volcano yet to blow and it will be bad."

"Maybe it's another Toba, the volcano was huge. But science disputes science, so I can only speculate," Clarity said. "After all unless we were there seventy-five thousand years ago on our planet when it erupted how could we know? Yet we are here. You are here and our earth exists."

"Why did you choose to stay here?" Menace asked. "Why not continue on?"

"I am searching for a female that came through a sinkhole. She was not on the planet those in the plane travel to. The mark you see on my shoulder appeared shortly after she did. She vanished before I could find out what it is. I don't know why but I will find out. The female changed me."

"How?" Solace asked.

Chaos gazed at her and she shivered. "There is a pull that is driving me. A presence of sorts that protects me."

Clarity leaned toward him to study the mark. "This could be anything but I think it's a key."

"To what?" Many chimed in.

"I don't know," Clarity said. "Why do you think you are protected?"

"Strange happenings occur when I appear to be in danger."

"Such as?" Lochlan asked.

"That plane almost landed on me. It was brought to me I have no doubt because of the alien. I had little clue what a plane was until I saw it for the first time. I am definitely protected, perhaps with a little too much enthusiasm. Last moment, I was pulled up onto a wing, the plane never touched down. We were sent up into the air after I was dragged inside. We landed here. Since we touched down, here is where I'm meant to stay, for now. Something is coming here, or is here. Something big."

"Something bad?" Menace asked.

"I'm uncertain," was Chaos's reply.

Solace had a strange feeling in her gut. She knew their world changed again. Something told her they would begin a new journey and would be walking with Chaos. After the thought, her tummy rumbled and she felt the stirring of life, only harder. Goosebumps rose on her arms. Without a doubt in her mind, she knew her new babies were going to be involved in something spectacular and maybe something sinister.

"Menace," she whispered.

He gripped her to him. "Are the babies all right?" he asked.

Menace placed a hand on her belly and jumped when movement fluttered within.

"It's all right Menace, the babies are supposed to move. You'll feel more later, especially since there are two."

"What's wrong?" Clarity asked.

"It's a feeling I have," Solace said. "What if the alien gave us these babies?"

"No." Clarity smiled. "Those babies are Menace's, have no worry. They are as much Menace's as my baby will be Doom's."

"What?" Doom yelled.

Rex slapped a little hand to his head. The hyena farted, and Bubble-gum played dead. All three cubs rolled onto the ground with their feet in the air in perfect imitation of their father.

"I'm gonna be sick," Clarity said and placed a hand over her mouth.

Menace clapped Doom on the back. "Welcome to my world, Daddy."

What a world it had become.

C.L. Scholey

About the Author

I love to write about everything and can't wait for an idea that grips me and sends me to a new place. Between worlds keeps me busy, that and chasing after my children and grandchildren. Plus one ornery one-hundred-sixteen pound mastiff who thinks he's a lap dog. Welcome into my adventures, and hang on!

~*~

Visit C.L. at

http://clscholey.com

~*~

To chat with C.L. Scholey and other Wild Rose Press authors of erotic romance, join us at

www.groups.yahoo.com/group/thewilderroses.

Also Available

Clarity's Doom
Ancient Origins Book 1

by

C.L. Scholey

http://a.co/0kry94c

A massive sinkhole phenomenon strikes terror on Earth and brilliant soon-to-be science graduate Clarity is sucked into a vortex that lands her on an alternate Earth planet where hybrid dinosaurs inhabit lush jungles. When caught in a fierce storm, she's rescued by the most magnificent alpha male with a serene yet hypnotic gaze she's ever encountered. As stunningly handsome as he might be, Clarity is no one's fool. There is deception in his intense gaze.

A warrior marked by death, an executioner by force, Doom leads the victims of sinkhole gatherings to slaughter. Each tattoo adorning his flesh depicts a sad tale of loss, a burden he must bear. But when he finds Clarity, she's spunky and filled with a determination he's never before encountered. Something inside him rises to meet her challenge to save his people, his very soul. He'll protect her at any cost, even if it means his life.

Also Read

Timeless Heat

by

Susanna Eastman

http://a.co/amfvLAc

Adrift in space after a strange cosmic phenomena sent them into severe sexual heat, intergalactic trader Joran Zoma and his business partner, Max, are dying. Time is running out, and only a woman from the distant past can save them.

Ava Fisher, recently divorced and deeply unhappy, is trying to move away from the hurt and bitterness of her past. Then she's kidnapped by two strangers— aliens from a different time and place. More astounding is their claim that she carries a rare hormone and must mate with them to save their lives.

Thank you for purchasing this
publication of The Wild Rose Press, Inc.
If you enjoyed the story, we would appreciate
your letting others know by leaving a review.
For other wonderful stories, please visit our
on-line bookstore at www.wilderroses.com.

For questions or more
information contact us at
info@thewildrosepress.com.

The Wild Rose Press, Inc.
www.thewilderroses.com

Stay current with The Wild Rose Press, Inc.
Like us on Facebook
https://www.facebook.com/TheWildRosePress
And Follow us on Twitter
https://twitter.com/WildRosePress